switch

switch

switch

tish cohen

harper*trophy*canada™

an imprint of harpercollins*publishers*ltd

Switch
Copyright © 2011 by Tish Cohen.
All rights reserved.

Published by Harper*Trophy* Canada™,
an imprint of HarperCollins Publishers Ltd.

First published in Canada in an original trade paperback edition by
Harper*Trophy* Canada™: 2011
This digest paperback edition: 2012

Harper*Trophy* Canada™ is a trademark of HarperCollins Publishers.

HarperCollins books may be purchased for educational, business, or sales promotional use through our Special Markets Department.

HarperCollins Publishers Ltd
2 Bloor Street East, 20th Floor
Toronto, Ontario, Canada
M4W 1A8

www.harpercollins.ca

Library and Archives Canada Cataloguing in Publication
information is available upon request

ISBN 978-1-55468-802-9

Printed in the United States
IMS 9 8 7 6 5 4 3 2 1

To my parents, Patricia Gill
and Lachlan Mackinnon Bleackley

chapter 1

Despite what Mr. Mansouri says, I didn't drive my mother's three-day-old station wagon through Sunnyside High School at lunchtime on a Tuesday as a childish plea for attention. I did it because I have thirty-seven siblings. Give or take. It's surprisingly hard to keep track. I mean, it's not as if we've all lived under the same roof at the same time. There are laws against that kind of thing. Or there seriously should be.

Sitting on the desk in front of me is a sheet of paper that demands to know the following: the date, my name, my homeroom teacher and the reason I'm in detention. Simple:

November 7th
Andrea Birch
Mrs. Coffey

Okay. The reason I'm in detention is complicated.

"I'm waiting, Miss Birch." Mr. Mansouri sits at the front of detention room. He leans back in his chair and puts his feet on the desk and right away I am sad and annoyed. Not by the act itself, but because of the way he crossed one foot over the other like a big shot. I mean, his loafers are all worn and decrepit and one of the heels is covered in flattened gum that's been stuck there so long it's turned black. Which makes them pretty unsuitable as the footwear of a big shot. That explains the sad. What makes me annoyed is that he went and made me feel sad for him in the first place.

He sees me looking and adds, "It shouldn't take long to complete the form if you tell the truth about what happened."

The truth.

Honestly, the truth is pretty long. I'm not sure it'll even fit on this sheet of paper. Or if I have the energy to get into it. That many brothers and sisters—even if they aren't blood relatives—is hard to explain.

See, my parents take in foster kids. Temporarily offer them a safe, loving haven from their horrifically broken lives. Or, more like my mom does. My dad does the loving haven thing part-time because he goes to work all day as a bank manager, then comes home to make sure the fosters have done their homework and chores. Once everyone's completed duties have been checked off on the laminated chart he keeps on the fridge, he changes into his baby-blue jeans and T-shirt and sheepskin slippers so he can monitor meteorological disturbances that hardly ever happen from the family room of our ranch bungalow. Since we live in Orange County, California—Fullerton, to be exact—the weather is pretty much sun, sun and more sun.

Which also makes me sad. I mean, if anyone, anywhere, was meant to be a weatherman it's Gary Birch. My father is a man without a storm. In Ugg slippers.

If you're thinking I have a pathetic issue with footwear, don't waste your brain cells. Mansouri having gum on his shoe and not knowing it is sad, no matter what my dad has on his feet.

Anyway, back to the fosters. It always starts the same way. They get dropped off by someone official—usually this woman who wrings her hands a lot and wears flowered pants—and they stay for a day, a year, sometimes half a decade. Then, as unexpectedly as my pretend siblings show up, they're gone. Either they're shipped back to parents who have kicked the drugs or been freed from prison, or else they're permanently adopted into loving homes. There's one constant with these pseudo brothers and sisters of mine. They leave.

They always, always leave.

My mother is a woman who never sits down. Seriously. It's entirely possible that her knees don't bend. Lise Birch is an MBA from Pepperdine who, before I was born, spent her days as a management consultant up in L.A. But she was fostered as a child for a few years when Gran got hooked on pain meds (more on Gran later, I promise), and Mom always wanted to give back. So after I was born, she went into the fostering game full-time, bringing in a pair of toddler brothers the day I turned one.

Mom never gets tired, never complains, is never too busy to wrap a lonely foster child in hugs, and never misses out on her bedtime routine of storytime by the gas fireplace, no matter how hot it is outside.

She is the quintessential perfect mother.

Except to me.

Don't get me wrong. She's not mean. Not even close. I am the lucky one, her "Number One," she insists. It's not that she doesn't care about my problems, either, but given that I was privileged enough to have been born to two pretty decent people, there's this underlying expectation that my emotional resilience is as fluffy and thick as the duvet folded neatly at the foot of my brass daybed. An air current runs through our house on Highcliffe Court. Andrea Birch is no sapling that buckles every time the jet stream changes course. She can handle it. Whatever "it" happens to be.

Take today. Auditions for the twelfth-grade spring fashion show were being held in the auditorium at lunch. I'm no stunner or anything, and there's probably no way I'd have been chosen, but I am in twelfth grade and thought it might be fun to try out. It's not as if it was going to pad my application to Stanford University, but I thought "why not?" Besides, the local stores offer up their newest fashions, and rumor is the models get to keep an entire outfit. Take one look inside my closet and you'll realize what that means to a girl like me, whose parents believe looking good is a sign of the Apocalypse. Just once, I'd like to step onto campus wearing designer jeans and cool boots I don't have to share with the fosters. Just once I'd like to turn a few heads, feel special.

If that makes me shallow, well, sorry. Try existing one week as me.

Not that I'm going to live this way forever. I got the letter this morning—from Mortimer Wolf, the recruiter from Stanford who's coming to interview applicants from my area on November 17th. That's this Wednesday—two days from now. At 1:25, I'll be sitting in one of the orange plastic chairs in Principal McCluskey's office, making sure Mortimer Wolf sees me as the perfect Stanford student. Here's the plan—get accepted with a full scholarship and, in nine months, next September, move four hundred miles north to Palo Alto, where I can escape all that it means to be Andrea Birch.

Anyway, I'd been practicing walking all sexy and coltish, leading with my hips like runway models do, in my room for a week. But as I ran out the door for the bus, Mom stopped me. Handed me the keys to her three-day-old Volvo and said there was an order ready for pickup at the drugstore and could I do it at lunch. She needed baby formula for the little girls' 4:30 feeding.

I could have argued, but come on. My mother, who had been up half the night because Kaylee was teething, was standing at the door with Kaylee's twin, Kaia, in her arms—the Ks are two chubby, pink, huggable babies whose favorite word is "Mama," even though their mother is a prostitute who turned tricks in the living room while the girls slept in their crib down the hall. Was I really supposed to tell Mom no? That I'd shaved my legs extra carefully and was planning to slip on platform stilettos and a pair of dark-rinse skinnies and let my hips pull me across Leighton Auditorium for an audience full of ogling boys?

I took the keys and promised to be home by 3:15.

Which, judging from the look on Mr. Mansouri's face, is not going happen. So here I sit. In detention hall, with a piece of paper that wants a better reason for why I'm being detained than the fact that I have thirty-seven foster sibs.

"I am waiting, Miss Birch." Mr. Mansouri sucks from a can of Coke. "The truth should come to you as quickly as your name."

I watch as he finishes the drink, crushes the can and tosses it at the trash. He misses, which makes me wince. If only to make him feel like the big shot he so badly wants to be, I click my pencil and give the man what he has asked for, sort of. The abbreviated truth.

I am in detention because of Joules Adams's red shirt.

Do I dare leave it at that?

I look down at the shirt. The chest is all stretched

out from where Joules's breasts were just three hours prior. And it's a terrible red. Any other red, a deep pepperoni or a faded tomato, for instance, might have had me in the Volvo right now, sucking back the new car smell, and Joules Adams doing whatever it is daughters of aging rock superstars do once the last bell rings.

But this red . . . I don't know what Joules was thinking. Seriously, if you're going to fool around with someone in the hedges between the student parking lot and the soccer field after lunch, and if that someone happens to be your boyfriend's best friend, Shane, and if said boyfriend is lacing up his soccer cleats straight across the field from you, you'll want to avoid a scarlet so dazzling it calls to mind an artery spurting neon-bright blood.

Mr. Mansouri booms as he picks up his soda can from the floor, "I'm waiting, Miss Birch. Your paper."

I look at my answer again and decide it's the best explanation I've got. So I underline it. Twice.

See, here's what went down . . . Joules was up to no good in the bushes. I was angelic in comparison— fresh from the drugstore, pulling the station wagon into the student parking lot, blissfully unaware of both the red shirt and the whatnottery in the shrubs. Lunch period was over, first bell had just rung. I was busy hunting for a parking spot in the shade where the infant formula would stay cool, hoping to get to the building where Honors English lives without hearing anything about who did or didn't make it as a fashion show model—and who would or would not be going home in my designer jeans.

Then it happened. The car door flew open and none other than Joules Adams was staring me in the face.

"Move over," she said, wiping shards of dead grass off her plaid skinnies and waving toward the passenger seat. Her bra strap was hanging through her sleeve and the red shirt was twisted sideways. But more bizarre was this—in the five years I've known her, it was the first time she'd spoken to me. "Move!"

Here's the thing about Joules. She's not exactly human. And the otherworldliness is not in her physical attributes—which, believe me, are astonishing enough. It's more in her patina. This polish of what I can only describe as authenticity that covers every inch of her being like fairy dust. It's like this magic powder that you feel, rather than see. There's not a store in the world that bottles it. Trust me, if there were, I'd be first in line. So would you.

Her long hair is so dark it's nearly black, except for these wavy ribbons of bronze that frame her face, which appears toasted all year round and is punctuated by lips the shape and color of a cinnamon heart. And gray eyes that blink about ten times slower than anyone else's. I don't really know why. I guess when you're Joules Adams you're never really in a hurry.

Believe me, life isn't going to leave this girl behind.

She's not the most popular girl in school. Not even close. That sort of designation is saved for the cheerleaders and the homecoming royalty and the cliquey chicks with the perma-sneers. No. Joules Adams doesn't have much in the way of friends. She's the kind of misfit you become if your dad is the only famous parent in the school. Contrary to what the average person might think, having a notorious parent does not make you revered, it makes you different. And different doesn't become a good thing until college. In high school, it's the kiss of social death.

I think she's the coolest girl in school.

And don't assume it's because her father is one of the biggest rock stars in the western hemisphere. I'm not that superficial. It's more like this: she's a loner because no one else is cool enough to hang in her

"I'll buy her another, I swear."

Surprisingly, that would not go over well in my house. "Yeah . . . my mother's big on the whole reduce, reuse, recycle thing so that's not really going to fly—"

I was slammed against my seat as the car lurched forward and roared through the student lot, barreling toward the teachers' parking.

It was then that I saw a quick flash of Brayden—my highly annoying fourteen-year-old foster brother, the longest foster we've ever had at five years and counting—and his three delinquent friends, smoking behind a tree that was doing very little to hide them. Even in my distress, I made a mental note to thump him later for cutting class and sucking nicotine with those losers.

At this point, Will was following us from behind, his shaggy brown hair blowing in the Santa Ana wind. Ms. Sylvester, the librarian, was pulling into the teachers' parking lot to our left. With the backside of the auditorium straight ahead, our only other escape route lay through the quad—a giant, paved patio area flanked by classrooms, gardens, outdoor tables and bike racks. My stomach flipped over as I realized what was about to happen.

Little Miss Rocker Girl was going to drive my mother's shiny green Volvo right through the school.

"No." My voice got embarrassingly high-pitched. You might even say shrieky. Verging on hysterical. "Joules . . . don't do it. Don't even think about it!"

I should explain. This is California, where classes are held in buildings that have outdoor hallways and lockers. Where, the rare day it rains, you need an umbrella to get from Algebra to English. Sunnyside High School looks like one huge, Spanish-style motel, with buildings that surround pretty parklands, sports fields and an open-air cafeteria. But there's one big difference.

No vehicles pull up to these doors.

Ever.

"Stop the car!" I set my hands on the dash and scanned the quad for teachers. Where was the administrative muscle when you needed it? The area was empty, except for a couple of stoners leaned up against a wall by the bathrooms. "You can't, you *cannot* drive this car through the school, Joules. Please tell me you have another plan."

My mother's words flashed through my mind: "I've waited my whole life for a Volvo, Andrea. It's my dream car. Practical, sturdy and long-lasting.

Remember, the cases of formula will be heavy—promise me you won't scratch the upholstery when you set them down."

The car veered right. I was flung against Joules's shoulder and, in the backseat, three cases of omega-three-infused Enfamil skidded across the leather seats and crashed into the door. There was a loud pop that could only have been a can of formula emptying itself onto the tan carpet. So much for new car smell. The station wagon lurched over the curb, thunking down again in the quad—where no vehicle dared go. When the DVD player dropped from the ceiling behind us and Dora the Explorer started singing, Joules looked over at me, wind blowing bronzed strands of hair in her face. "I have no other plan."

"Then stop the car," I shouted over the engine and Dora's annoying voice. "Joules. Stop the freaking car!"

She made a sharp left into an arched hallway at the far end of the quad, and as she screeched to a halt, the back end swung out from behind us like something out of *Dukes of Hazzard*.

Finally, Joules turned around to look at the interior of the car, her cheeks flushed and sweating, her black ponytail swinging, her gold nose ring glinting in the sun. I was struck by the fact that the one and only thing we had in common at that moment, besides both being students at Sunnyside, was long, dark hair pulled into ponies. She looked at the running shoes in the backseat, the *Hop on Pop* book in the passenger door. "So, what? You have a big family?"

I was still trying to catch my breath. "Yeah."

Her eyes took in the double-sided photo of Kaylee and Kaia hanging from Mom's rearview mirror and she allowed herself a tiny smile. "Lucky," she said.

Lucky.

Me.

Then the moment was broken. "Switch tops with me, Birch Tree. Then Will thinks it was you back there with Shane."

"Me? Why would I want—?"

"*Pleasepleasepleasepleaseplease.*"

Crap. Not only did I not want to strip down in the quad, but she was talking about my favorite shirt. I saved for two months for that top. I was careful not to wear it around the fosters all year, and it was the only thing I owned that wasn't covered in battery acid or grape juice stains.

To be honest, I started to rethink the whole sharing-cookies-at-lunch thing.

"I'm begging you, Birchie. I adore Will. He's my Reason-for-Breathing." In the side mirror I saw Will jogging across the quad toward us.

Here's the thing about Will Sherwood. I've had a silent but deadly crush on him since we were eight and sitting cross-legged in assembly one morning at Poplar Plains Elementary. He was behind me and said, "You're sitting on my shoelace." Which I was. I mumbled sorry and shifted to free his black sneakers, and he said, "It's alright." Just like that, "It's alright." There was no hidden emotion in his words or anything (believe me, I hunted for it). But any other boy would have given me a shove or said something idiotic like, "Yeah, I'd be sorry too if I had your face." Not Will. Will excused me, and for that I started to take a closer look at him.

Trouble is, I've never been able to look away.

"Here?" I asked Joules. "You want to trade shirts right *here*?"

"I will totally owe you." She pulled a CD partway out of her purse. Nigel Adams.

"Is that the new one?"

She nodded. "Signed."

I'd have to hide it from Brayden—who's obsessed with Nigel Adams. "Fine. But I want my shirt back tomorrow."

We pulled off our tops and swapped, and right away she climbed out of the car. I was free. As fast as I could, I hopped back into the driver's seat, turned around and started to back the car toward the safety and normality of the parking lot, where I planned to re-assume control of my life.

That's when I saw it. Mr. Mansouri's bald head glistening in the sun, flashing in my eyes like an SOS signal as he ran toward us from the metal shop. Sweet relief—I'd never been so happy to see a hairless cranium in my life. As ridiculous as it was, I almost felt sorry for Joules. Mansouri would surely pulverize her for what essentially amounted to the following:

carjacking
driving a motor vehicle through a school full
   of minors
kidnapping an innocent student (a Stanford-
   bound honor student!)
and crushing the dream of a friendship that
   could have brought a tiny amount of joy to
   my days.

In that moment, my mind raced through all that might happen to her. Suspension. Expulsion. Prison.

I hoped, though, they wouldn't go that far. In fact, I determined right then and there to refuse to testify on the kidnapping charge.

I thrust the car into park and climbed out, exhausted. Relieved. Ready to negotiate a lesser punishment for Joules, whom I'd already begun to dislike for making me feel as sorry for her as I would later for Mansouri. Seriously. Her student record was going to be wrecked. *Wrecked.*

Mansouri's words puffed out in time with his crashing footsteps. "Andrea Birch . . . have you ever . . . seen a motor vehicle . . . of any kind . . . on this campus?" He slowed as he got close, holding his chest and leaning over to catch his breath. "EVER?"

"I know, right?" I started to say. "It's a good thing no kids were around—"

He pointed at me, then his metal shop. "Your carcass in my class after school. Don't even think about being late."

"What? Me?" I spun around to stare at Joules, who was now standing arm in arm with a relieved-looking Will, running her fingers through the deliciously tangled mop of hair that framed his face. "*I* wasn't driving the car."

"Don't you try to get out of this!" Mansouri

19

roared. "I saw that fire-engine color from clear across campus."

Sigh. See what I mean about the red?

"No . . ." I looked to Joules for help, but her pony-tailed head was resting on Will's chest and she was rubbing his soccer bib, completely at peace with herself. I couldn't come out and say it was Joules's shirt. It would end things for her and Will. And as much as I'd like that, I do have a heart. No designer jeans—and maybe no place to live once my mother sees the Volvo's ruined carpet—but plenty of heart. I also have a guiding principle: I refuse to be the cause of any kind of pain in Will Sherwood's life. Besides, let's face it, the Andrea–Will crush is nothing if not one-sided. Breaking them up will not send him running after me.

"3:05," Mansouri bellowed. "Be there. Miss Adams, you too."

"Me?" Joules's voice rose into the high-pitched squawk of the wrongly accused. "I had no idea she'd drive through the school like that, Mr. Mansouri . . ."

He stared at me. "And, Miss Birch, a word of advice. Next time you're driving a getaway vehicle with plans to foist your involvement onto another soul when you get caught, take the time, pre-caper, to dress yourself in a more subdued hue. I'll see you after school."

Now, in detention, wiping grass off the red shirt I planned to burn later, wondering if I was crazy to take the heat for a girl who may or may not give me that CD, I look through the open door to see Joules standing very close to her (and my) Reason-for-Breathing. She's in no rush to report to Mansouri, that's for certain. They talk for a moment, then Will smiles a blushing, dimple-making kind of smile that makes me tingle down to my toes. He glances down, then back up at her again. Then, in a movement surely designed to rip out my heart, he reaches up, tenderly, lovingly, to swipe a strand of hair from her face.

Mom calls me The Lucky One. But she has no idea what she's talking about. She's never met Joules Adams.

I hand my detention sheet to Mr. Mansouri and return to my seat. He pushes his wire-rimmed glasses up his nose, examines my response and slaps the paper down on his desk. "So, the only thing you did wrong was getting seen, Miss Birch? Is that your belief?"

Lying is so not my style. Getting in trouble is so not my style. But Will Sherwood is. So I shrug. "There weren't any actual signs posted. You know, saying cars weren't allowed."

A flush of magenta creeps up from his shirt collar. "That's fine. If that's the way you want to play it. But I'm watching you. Make no mistake about it—you are officially on my radar."

I nod, horrified. Humiliated.

Finally, a full ten minutes late, Joules saunters in. All plaid skinnies and knee-high Docs and my white shirt straining across her chest. She drops into the seat in front of me and slides down low. Right away she starts carving something in the edge of the desk. I lean sideways to watch the initials *JA* appear in the wood.

I poke her in the back. "When do I get my shirt back?"

"Keep mine."

"I don't want to keep yours. I want mine."

"Don't get all bent. It's a wad of cotton." Her phone buzzes and she checks it. Giggles to herself, then turns around to show me a text from Nigel61. Her dad.

what—my jujube wasn't driving? shame, girlie. grounded
6 wks.

"You're grounded?" I ask, kind of impressed with
her dad.

She looks at me as if I'm an idiot. "He's joking,
Birch Tree." Giggling, she whispers to herself, "Dad's
such a geek." Joules yawns and stands up. Fishes
something out of her bag and walks to the front,
dragging her boots. She slaps a CD—*my CD!*—on
Mansouri's desk.

He picks it up. "This the new one?"

"Not released in stores till next month. Signed,
too. Check out the back."

He flips it over, nodding. "My estranged daughter
thanks you."

Great. Why did he have to say that? Does he not
realize some of us are going to wonder and worry
about why his daughter won't speak to him unless
he coughs up swag? And what does he mean by
estranged? Does she see him at all? Does he spend
his birthday with nothing to keep him company but
the shine of his head and the gum on his shoe? And
why does she have to avoid him anyway—does she
not see the way his shoes are so worn at the heels?
Does that not make her just the tiniest bit sad?

Mansouri looks up at Joules and nods toward the door. "Get going before I change my mind."

With a cute nose-scrunching smile back at me, and with no remorse about giving away the CD, Joules heads out the door. Through the window, I see Will wave her over to the soccer field. She races up and tackles him, rolling him around on the turf, surely getting grass stains on my shirt. I look away before they lock lips.

Seeing that might just kill me.

chapter 2

My stomach slithers down to my hips as I pull the Volvo into our driveway. There's Mom, on the porch, arms folded across her chest, leaning against the open door, short, grayish hair fluttering away from her face, not daring to get in her eyes.

I glance at the dashboard: 4:45. I'm an hour and a half late.

There's a thing my mother does with her mouth when she's mad. She purses her lips as if she's sucking on a smoke—something she would never do—and if you look really close, you'll see her upper lip twitch. Tiny nerve endings fire like furious little pistons. When it happens, all of us kids, big or small, blood relations or treasured charges, Lucky Number One or Number Thirty-five, know to disappear.

I can see the twitch all the way from the driveway as she watches me haul the three busted cases of

Enfamil out of the car and up the front steps. Which means one thing: she knows.

I step up onto the porch and Mom says nothing.

"I had detention," I say, with a world-weary sigh.

One of the boxes shifts. There's a creak and a tearing sound, and three cans of formula drop onto the concrete veranda and start to roll. One starts to hiss, and thick beige liquid chugs out and pools at Mom's feet.

"I heard. This is really not like you, Andrea."

"I know! The whole thing is completely circumstantial . . ."

But her attention has already turned to the Volvo. She marches down the steps and starts opening up the car doors. I silently beg her not to look in the backseat or she's certain to see—

"There's baby formula all over the rugs back here! I don't believe it!" She stares back at me. "Were you in some kind of an accident?"

"No, I . . . there's this girl, Joules. I guess she's kind of wild. She's, you know, her dad is that rocker guy who lives up on Skyline . . ."

Mom starts back toward the steps. "And this, all this today, is the result of a friendship with a wild girl?" She stops in front of me and sets her hands on her hips. "Doesn't sound like the kind of friend I'd like to have. You might want to reconsider who you hang around with on a daily basis."

Okay. I have been decidedly anti-Joules since she jumped in the car, but hearing Mom write her off as no kind of friend makes me want to be Joules's best friend forever. "She's not that bad. It all had to do with this guy, Will."

"Mr. Mansouri told me all about it. How you'd been fooling around in the bushes with one of the Enderby boys and somehow this Joules was involved and the two of you used my Volvo—my three-day-old Volvo!—as a getaway car. Then you scrawled some sort of joke across the detention sheet? I'd say any girl who inspired a transformation like this is pretty bad."

"Wait, how do you know about Shane?"

"That's not important. What's important is—"

"I wasn't in the bushes with Shane or any other boy!"

She takes a case of formula from my arms and starts inside. "Enough. We'll talk about this later. We'll also talk about what this does to our reputation as a family. And to my reputation as a caregiver."

"This? What about Samantha and Cici getting

into Dad's car when they were nine and ten, and driving it halfway up the block? What about Brayden breaking into the Millers' with Tomas and Dillon and Ace and flooding their bathrooms? Wait—did Brayden tell you about Shane? Because if he did, he got it all wrong."

"I said we'll talk about it later. After the babies are fed and the rugs in the car are shampooed." She looks back at me. "By you."

"Okay." The cases are cutting into my biceps, so I shimmy past her and into the kitchen. The twins are in their high chairs waiting for their 4:30 feeding. I set the cases on the counter and pour formula into two glass bottles that are all set up, sterilized and ready to go, then warm some water in a small pot. When it's partway heated, I stick the bottles in.

Kaylee and Kaia start kicking their edible chubster legs as they watch me. How anyone could give birth to these two and then treat them like stale donuts just kills me. They're nearly impossible to look away from. Seriously, some mornings when they toddle into the kitchen in their footsie pajamas, with their thumbs in their drooly mouths and sleepy eyes all wide and astonished, I can barely bring myself to go to school.

Here's the trouble with human babies. They're dependent on their parents for too long—way longer than any other species. Plus the whole being-born thing is like Russian roulette. A kid can be born to a rock star like Nigel Adams, who forks over major bucks to charities and is super-cool to his daughter in detention, or to the loser with a spare evening on her hands, with nothing more to qualify her to care for a child than a cold beer and a hot date. Unborn babies should be afraid, very afraid, of whom they'll meet once they scrabble their way out of the womb.

It's the kind of thing that hits me at three in the morning. The randomness of it all.

Mom crosses the room and pulls one of the bottles from the pan, shakes formula on her wrist to check the temperature. Satisfied, she takes both bottles over to the chortling babies, who've caught sight of their treasures and are reaching out with tiny saliva-covered fingers and bopping up and down in their seats. In unison, they push silicone teats into red mouths, closing their eyes and sighing with relief as they start to suck and swallow. If Mom weren't so mad at me, it would be the most delicious moment on earth.

Brayden appears from nowhere, all braces and bouncy yellow curls and buffalo plaid shirt. He grins

29

as he pokes me in the gut. "So, Enderby, huh? He once did it with a lunch lady. Nice score!"

"How did you even hear?"

"How could I not hear?" He thumps me in the chest. "The whole school knows, MANdrea."

I shove him backward. "Yeah? Well, check your facts next time, Bray!"

He loses his footing and falls against the oven, then lets himself flop onto the floor where he fakes his death. After a moment, he puffs out his mouth as if he's hiding a strawberry in there, but what he's really hiding is laughter because the whole tumble was staged. He groans in Mom's direction. "See what she did to me?"

"Don't play people for sympathy, Brayden," says Mom. "You never want to wheedle love out of anyone. You're better than that."

Bray ignores Mom and throws a useless kick in my direction. "She's verbally abusing a foster child. Didn't you tell her I was born a crack baby?"

Mom leans down to pull him upright. As her hand caresses his hair, he winks at me. "You are not your history, Brayden Jacob Green. Don't ever use it like that, not even as a joke. You are loved. Do you know why?"

"Why?"

She squishes his face between her hands and kisses his nose. "Because you are a wonderful human being and you are worthy of affection." She spins him around and swats his behind. "Now go take your turn in the shower before the girls get home and hog the bathroom."

He walks out slowly, letting each leg stomp out in front of him as he passes me by, grinning. "Okay, *Mom*."

I look at Mom, appalled. Brayden has broken the Mom/Lise, Dad/Gary rule. Only I—as Number One of thirty-seven—am allowed to call Mom and Dad "Mom and Dad." This, besides being the only one who has her own room, is my one privilege as a full-blooded Birch. The others have to say Lise or Gary. They *have* to say Lise or Gary. It's a rule.

"Mom," I say. "He didn't call you Lise!"

"Sorry, Lise." Brayden turns around at the doorway and makes sad puppy eyes at her. "Sometimes I forget I wasn't born to you."

"I put in an order for you, funny boy," Mom calls out from the stove. "You just came to me a different way."

Ugh. For a moment I debate telling Mom I saw

him smoking as Joules and I whizzed past the shop buildings, but I figure it will only incriminate me even more.

Mom turns back to the high chairs to release the toddlers into their playpen, conveniently missing Brayden mooning me from down the hall. I stomp threateningly in his direction and he disappears, the bathroom door slamming shut behind him.

"As for you, Andrea . . ." She motions for me to follow her down the hall, where she tugs a rusted metal cot from the closet, complete with a blue-striped mattress folded inside. Then she pulls out a stack of sheets and plunks them in my arms. "Come with me."

I do, as she pushes the squeaking cot all the way down to my bedroom door.

"We need your room." She bumps my door open with her hip and announces, like it's a good thing, that my furniture needs to be pushed to one corner.

"What? But what about our rule? My room is my room because I'm your Number One and all that. Because I'm so, so lucky. Right? Remember—no one is allowed in my room without my permission. That is our rule, right? Andrea's room is Andrea's room. No one invades it."

"You broke a few major rules today, so I'm not sure you want to bring up rules just now. Reality is, we're clear out of space."

"No, we're not! Brayden has his room and the girls have the other. The babies are with you. We're fine."

I watch her roll the cot to where my desk sits, along with my bulletin board and adored bookshelves I worked so hard to make out of plywood and bricks left over from the patio Dad built.

"Mom, you can't do this! It's the way I keep sane. My room is all I have and—"

She stands up and frowns at me. "I think we can do without the dramatics, darlin'. Your life looks pretty good from where I'm standing."

My wind comes fast and furious and I fight not to stop breathing altogether. "What are you talking about? I'm an afterthought around here!"

"Have you ever been left in your crib while your crack-addict mother went out to score? Have you been hit? Starved? Left with a pervert uncle?"

I can't help but make a joke here. "Well, Uncle Jimmie likes to watch his pornos. One time when I was staying over, I snuck down to get some cookies—"

33

"I am being serious, Andrea. These kids come from garbage situations. They've had garbage lives. You know that. I sincerely hope that temporarily sharing your room is the very worst thing that ever happens to you. I sincerely do."

This silences me. I watch as she starts sliding books from my shelves and stacking them on the floor. Above her, pinned to my bulletin board, is the letter from the Stanford recruiter, Mortimer Wolf. *Be patient for now,* I tell myself. *It's less than a year until September.* I drop to my knees and help her, cradling my Judy Blumes and my Harry Potters and my Bellas and Edwards close to my chest, trying not to cry. "Who's moving in—Samantha or Cici?"

"Neither. I have a bit of news."

"Oh no."

A bit of news is never good, not when it's coming from my mother's mouth. The first time she told me she had a "bit of news" was when I was about five. The news, which she assured me was all good, concerned Joshie and Drew, my six- and eight-year-old brothers, as I'd always known them, with whom I'd lived as long as my young memory served. Joshie and Drew helped me build a good-dreams-only tent over my bed when I was afraid of nightmares.

They taught me early on that it wasn't cool to watch *Teletubbies*. They showed me how to wiggle my ears. And they were being adopted into a "loving home."

I just sat in the bath that day, stunned. Adopted? Into a loving home? What was wrong with our home? Did we not love them?

Mom tried to explain but I was inconsolable. You can't fling terms like "temporary situation" and "long-term childcare agreements" at a five-year-old covered in Mr. Bubble. Words like these mean nothing to her.

My brothers—with whom I'd shared every cold, every game of tag, every Disney movie, every trip to Laguna Beach—were leaving and I was never to see them again. It was the last time I ever thought of the fosters as my real siblings. Mom can call them whatever she wants, but the truth is they aren't related to me. The truth is, each and every one will go away.

Tell me *you* wouldn't start to distrust "a bit of news."

Mom gives me a sad smile. "We have a new girl coming tonight, very last minute. It's a terrible situation."

"They're all terrible situations. We don't have room for any more kids!"

"Sometimes you open your door anyway."

"*My* door. Aren't there laws about this? Foster kids sharing rooms and stuff?"

"Kids have shared rooms since the beginning of time. Anyway, there's nowhere else for her to go right now. While she's with us, she'll be the number-one focus of our lives."

Number One? With my room gone, with the Mom/Lise, Dad/Gary rule shattered, wasn't that all I had left?

Last summer, a reporter showed up from the *Orange County Sun*. Brought a photographer, even. Wanted to do a human interest piece, so he interviewed Mom, of course, and a few of the kids. But mostly he was interested in me. Freak-show me. "What's it like to be number one of thirty-eight kids?"

Oy, I thought. Where to start?

See, when you're me, you're never really me. Me is stained by what's around me. And by "what's around me" I mean the other kids in my house. This is how I explained it to the guy.

All the houses in our neighborhood look pretty much the same. The ranch bungalows might come in a few different shapes, but most have the same tan-and-brown trim color, same taupe stucco, same

white concrete driveway, same tropical leafery leading up to the walk, same three-car garage, same leafy
eucalyptus trees lining each street. They're your typi-
cal Southern California tract homes, and whoever
constructed our subdivision built quite a few others
around town using the exact same plans. Someone
might make the mistake of thinking the houses are
the same inside, too. But they aren't. The lives inside
make each house very different, and a few years ago
ours became notorious. It became "the house with
all the trouble."

And as the number of kids who moved in and
out grew, it wasn't just the house's reputation that
changed. Mine did too. I became a local curios-
ity. A smash-up on the side of the freeway. When-
ever I passed the white-haired couple at number
8414—the ones who wore golf pants and matching
visors, who pruned their trees so they never grew
taller than the house—one would start to nudge
the other and, together, they'd give me these stony
looks. Extreme disapproval. Like it was my fault the
police cars pulled up when Brayden ran away, or
like it was me—not Samantha or Cici, now twelve
and thirteen—who got caught shoplifting sparkly
blue nail polish and Dentyne and magazines from

the drugstore, to be chauffeured home in the police cruiser yet again. Like I was the delinquent.

The reporter pushed his glasses up his nose. "But what's it really like? On a day-to-day basis, being Number One?"

I looked to see if Mom was out of earshot and pulled my chair closer. And I told him.

I told him about the lineup for the bathroom in the morning—so long sometimes that I'd sneak out into the yard to pee.

I told him that every time Brayden or, before him, Marky or Kyle or Daniel, ran away, the police would search my room—my diary, even!—for clues to his whereabouts.

I told him that my allowance was ridiculously low because the fosters need money for comic books, T-shirts or forty-ouncers of rum (the reporter thought I was kidding about that, but he'd never seen Marky's fake ID).

Very few of my comments made it into the paper. What did make it onto page seven was Mom's proud story of how my training bra was worn by thirteen girls other than me, and counting. I got teased at school for a whole year.

The piece was called "Child One of Thirty-Eight."

I wonder, sometimes, what it would be like to be interviewed for an article with this title: "Child One of One."

Stanford University, Palo Alto, California . . . here I come.

•

The grandfather clock beside Dad's chair bongs eight times and he pushes back the sleeve of his shirt to synchronize his watch to the clock, which is set to Universal Time, a time scale based on the mean solar day—and what he believes to be the most accurate measure of time in the world. Things like this are important to fathers like mine. As he stabs at the tiny buttons on his Seiko, he glances up at me and Brayden, side by side on the sofa where Mom placed us, and half smiles, his mustache spreading across the lower half of his comfortably drooping face. When his watch is all synched up, he rubs the top of his reddish-grayish buzz cut and sits back to wait.

"They're calling for clouds tomorrow," he announces to fill the silence.

Brayden and I nod politely.

39

There's another rule in the Birch house. If you're home, if you're over five, you put on some clean clothes and sit in the living room like a respectable person when a new child arrives.

"Either of you two know where Samantha and Cici are?"

Brayden grunts. "Probably knocking over a liquor store."

Dad squints his disapproval. I elbow Brayden, who's busy examining his feet, just to make sure he knows he's being scowled at.

Just then, a clattering like thundering hooves comes down the hall and Cici's long, fuzzy red hair appears in the doorway. Her tank and shorts show off her long, lanky muscles (which she doesn't have to work for, by the way—the most exercise she gets is running out of the drugstore after having shoplifted a package of fake eyelashes). Sam, who appears beside her, could easily be on her way to a roller disco. Her short beige hair is pulled back in a gold headband and her purple stretch shorts are so skimpy they could double as undies.

The familiar smell of cotton candy lip gloss wafts toward me. Sure enough, both Sam and Cici are smacking freshly glossed lips—glossed with *my* lip gloss. From *my* room.

"You might as well keep it," I say.

"Keep what?" says Sam.

I motion toward my lips. "I'm not going to use it now."

"Sweet!" she squeals, and trots back to my room to pocket her latest score.

"We're just going out for ice cream," says Cici, flipping her hair. "Sam's dying for some rocky road."

Sam is back, reapplying my gloss. "Yup. Rocky road. Can't get enough."

Dad checks his watch again. "Not this late, you aren't. It's after eight. Besides, we have a new girl coming in a few minutes. You know what that means." He motions toward the empty sofa across the room. "All bottoms on deck."

"Just this once, Gary," says Sam. "Please? We won't even stay long."

"There'll be plenty of rocky road left tomorrow," Dad says.

Sam nudges Cici with her elbow and Cici blurts out, "Yeah, but there's this guy who works there and Sam totally has the hots for him and he only works 'til—"

"Don't go and say that, idiot!" Sam glares at her.

"What? I'm not going to lie about things like you do!"

"Oh, but stealing deodorant is fine?"

41

Dad stands up and guides the two of them by their elbows to the sofa. "Nobody in this house needs to steal deodorant. There's plenty to go around. You'll both sit here and welcome the new girl, just like the others greeted you when it was your turn. This is a rule that doesn't get bent."

Sam pouts as Dad points at the seat cushions. She makes a tragic face and falls onto the couch, dejected, then whispers, just quietly enough that Dad doesn't hear, "Thanks for ruining my life."

So here we sit, all five of us, cleaned up and staring at each other like goons, and wait for Mom to finish up out front with the woman from Child Services. The one with the flowered pants.

Brayden has our fanciest pillow on his lap and starts braiding the gold tassels. I poke him in the thigh because one of the tassels is starting to unravel and it's important for a family to have at least some nice things.

"Low pressure front moving in," says Dad. "Should be gone by Thursday."

"Thursday, huh?" says Brayden, trying not to smile. "Swee-eet."

I pinch him.

The front door creeps open and we all lean for-

42

ward to get a good look. Only it isn't Mom with the new girl; it's Gran, looking fierce in her spiked blond hair and black hipster reading glasses. She smiles at us. "Well, look at you people, all shined up like brand-new pennies."

Dad says, "Lise is bringing in a new—"

"I know, I know. That's why I'm here. Terrible what happened, isn't it? When I saw it on the news, I nearly cried. Just last night—and right in front of Disneyland!"

Dad shakes his head gravely and nods toward the rest of us, clearly hoping to shut her up.

"What happened?" I ask.

"Yeah, what happened?" says Sam.

"Lise wants to keep it quiet," Dad says. "You kids don't need to hear every gory detail about every person who crosses the threshold."

Brayden sits forward. "We sure do!"

"No, Gary's right," says Gran. "Forget I said anything. I've got some prezzies for you kids so you don't feel displaced by the new girl." She sets down a large gift bag that looks like it's been re-gifted a few times too many, pulls out two pink tubes and tosses one to Sam and the other to Cici. As they start to squeal in delight, I realize it's cotton candy lip gloss.

"Thanks!" says Sam.

"Awesome, Gran," says Cici.

In case you're wondering, there's no rule about Gran's name. Gran's Gran to pretty much everybody.

"I'm glad you like it. The salesgirl told me it will give you lips that are devastatingly kissable."

"Now, now," says Dad. "Sam and Cici don't need any encouragement."

"Don't be ridiculous, Gary. Young girls love to primp." To Brayden, she tosses the latest issue of *Spin* magazine.

"Sick!"

"You're welcome," Gran says, frowning. "I think."

Next she pulls something black and floppy from the bag and hides it behind her back. Uh-oh. I don't like the way she's beaming at me. It's making me think my gift is going to make me anything but devastatingly kissable. "And I have something extra-special for my granddaughter."

She drops a pair of crazy rubber gloves on my lap and takes a step back to wait for my reaction. And, honestly, I don't know how to react. Not only did she gift me with something made for doing menial labor, but the gloves are black with long silver nails painted on each fingertip, swirly crystal bedazzling up the wrists and all these freaky feathers at the top. I glance longingly at Cici and Sam, swiping yummy pink gloss across their already glossy lips.

"They're for doing dishes," Gran says. "To make it more fun. Try them on."

"Yeah, um . . ."

"I brought them all the way home from Africa. Don't you just love them?"

I slip my hands into the gloves and force a smile. "What's not to love?"

"I knew it. As soon as I saw them there, in the market, I thought of you."

"For sure." I mean, why would Andrea Birch want to be kissed?

"Of course, there's a wonderful story behind them."

With Gran, there's always a story. She found my sherpa hat on a ski lift in the Himalayas ("Can you imagine? Someone left it behind!"), she bought the batik skirt that comes down to my heels and is covered in teensy sequined butterflies at a bazaar in Malaysia, and the hand-carved wooden box she gave me for my jewelry (if you look really close, you can see the wavy pattern is actually two people humping, but

Gran doesn't believe me) is from a pawnshop in Des Moines. She bought it because it was rumored to have once belonged to Rosanna Arquette. Which it probably didn't.

Gran sits across from me and winks. "Take real good care of them. I picked them up in Africa just after my safari . . ."

Let me explain. Gran is a wild one. She takes cruises around remote parts of the world with her bachelor friend, Mr. Marcus. Two years ago, she received a bit of spam via e-mail. It was an ad for a river cruise through the jungles of Guatemala with a guide named River Jack, meals included. Mom and I begged her not to go—she knew nothing at all about this River Jack guy except what she'd read on his website. We told her he could be unstable, she could be killed. But Gran, being Gran, went anyway. River Jack did take Gran and Mr. Marcus through the jungle alright, and the meal was in a mud hut, prepared by his wife, Windy—a French woman with long, grizzled black hair who offered Gran a reading from the Guatemalan gods on a straw mat outside the hut. The night Gran returned home, she phoned to tell us: a) she'd had a great time, b) the Guatemalan gods told her to take valerian root to clear up her arthritis, and c) Mom and I should try to be a bit less paranoid when it comes to strangers because we'll wind up missing out on life.

The very next day, River Jack was actually on the news, right there on CNN. His boat—the very same leaky pontoon Gran and Mr. Marcus had been on the day prior—had been stormed by guerillas. The Swedish tourists on board were kidnapped, all five of them, and were being held at machete-point in an abandoned barn which was, at that very moment, surrounded by Guatemalan police.

Gran's response? Crime happens everywhere.

I'm spared Gran's latest crazy story when we hear Mom's voice from the porch.

Footsteps grow louder, then the door clicks. Creaks open. Mom walks into the living room so cautiously it's as if she's walking across a swinging bridge. In her arms, with bare arms and legs wrapped around her for dear life, is a small girl.

She's about six or so, wearing an old-fashioned yellow dress with puffed sleeves. It probably came down to her knees a few years back, but now it barely covers her underpants. Long grasshopper legs with freshly skinned knees dangle down, ending in frilled white socks and black party shoes. Her face is tucked into Mom's shoulder, but atop her neck, white-blond braids are coiled on either side of her head like Princess Leia's. One thing is certain, this girl isn't from around here.

"Everybody," Mom half whispers, as if the child might break if she speaks in a real voice, "this is Michaela. Michaela, this is Gary, Brayden, Andrea, Cici and Samantha. And Gran. You'll meet the little ones tomorrow."

"Oh my," whispers Gran, her eyes tearing up. "Just precious."

Without lifting her head up, Michaela steals a look at us, exposing an angry bruise above one eye, then tucks her chin into her cotton collar. When she doesn't make a sound, Mom motions me to follow her into the dim light of what used to be my room.

"She's exhausted" is all Mom says.

I want to know, but I don't want to know, what happened that was so bad it made it into the news. I mean, here's this kid with her fancy shoes and her hairdo and this bruise. Whatever went down, it wasn't good.

See? Luck of the draw. It's what our entire existence is based on—stupid, stupid luck.

Only a lamp on the wooden chair beside the cot

is lit. When Mom shows Michaela the carefully made up bed, the girl clings tighter to her neck. After Mom nods her approval, I loosen the party shoes and set them side by side on the floor, then Mom sits on the thick duvet and lowers Michaela onto the pillow. She tugs the covers out from under the child's legs and I pull them up to Michaela's chin. In the grainy darkness, her eyes open wide—I can't tell whether from fear or lack of light. Maybe both.

The phone rings from out in the hall and Michaela looks even more terrified. Mom tells her she's safe now. That nothing is going to hurt her. That she's in Andrea's room and should get a nice rest. As we back away, Michaela squeals like a frightened kitten.

Mom rushes back to kiss her braided head, but Michaela squeals again.

"I know what might help," I say to my mother. I grab an armload of stuffed animals off the foot of my bed—I'm miles too old for these, I know—and hold them in front of her. There's a stuffed giraffe from the San Diego Zoo. I got that when I was about nine. A pink cat wearing a sweat suit. A raggedy sock monkey that used to have buttons for eyes but now just has knotted black thread, and a floppy-eared dog with matted fur the color of a Kraft caramel. That one I got from Gran when I had my tonsils out. The story behind it was simpler than most. She picked it up for a quarter at a neighbor's garage sale.

Michaela ignores the menagerie and vanishes beneath the white sheets.

I look at my mom. "What happened to her?"

Mom shakes her head. "Better you don't hear it."

"Gran already said it was on TV, so you know I'll find out eventually."

Mom thinks about it a minute and guides me over to the window. She whispers, "Michaela and her parents were crossing the street, right in front of Disneyland." She stops to make sure Michaela is still beneath the sheets. Once assured the child cannot hear, she continues. "Hit by an SUV, both parents. Neither parent is conscious at this point. And the driver didn't even stop. Just took off. Left an entire family to maybe die right there on the street. There are roadblocks set up all over the city tonight. Looking for the vehicle."

"That's awful . . ."

"Yes, well. Unfortunately, there's a whole lot of awful out there."

The cotton moves. Mom and I turn to see tiny fingers appear with nails trimmed short. The sheets lift up and one blue eye is visible. Nothing happens for a second, then the hand shoots out, takes the garage sale dog by the tail and whisks him out of sight. Soon afterward, we hear deep, restful breathing.

Mom and I tiptoe out of the room, into the bright light of the hall. "Listen, Andrea. Don't tell the other kids. I don't want word to spread that the girl from the accident is staying here or the press might come sniffing around. Let's just keep it quiet. Okay?"

"Sure."

Brayden tears out of the living room and, in his tube socks, slides along the wooden floor and into my face.

"You had a phone call, Mandrea."

I stare at him a moment. He wants to get me riled up.

"Andrea," Mom sings a warning from farther down the hall. "Remember what I've told you . . ."

Of course. She says it's the broken kid in him. That he's had a tough life and I should handle this like an adult. Or a near-adult. It'll make him respect me. And once he respects me, our relationship will mature. Supposedly. It's worth a shot.

"Brayden, I would prefer you don't use that nickname. I find it offensive and demeaning. Do you understand why that would be?"

I hear Mom's approving footsteps walk away.

"Oh, I understand," says Bray.

"Good." I look at his smiling face. "This is good. Now, who was on the phone?"

"Some guy. I told him you were in the bathroom, and judging from the number of tacos you wolfed at dinner, our Mandrea would probably be tied up for quite a while."

Forget maturity. Forget understanding. Forget respect. I chase him down the hall and into his room, where he throws himself onto the bottom bunk and covers his boy parts with his pillow. I jump on top of him and grab him by the shirt collar. "Who was it, Braceface?"

He rolls out from under me and leans against a poster of Nigel Adams in pants made from a British flag. "Unhand me, Mandrea!"

"Fine." I sit back, tucking hair behind my ears. "Who was it?"

No answer.

"Who was it, Bray?"

He sits up, fusses with his shirt and squeaks, "You totally messed up my collar."

"WHO WAS IT?"

"Get off my bed or I'll never tell you."

I stand up and kick his mattress. "Do you want me to tell Dad I saw you and your goons smoking by the metal shop today? And cutting class?"

"I'll just say I was late for Phys Ed—because I was watching *you* drive across the freaking quad! And what were you doing with the hottest girl in school anyway?"

Brayden has had a crush on Joules for over a year now. Thinks she's about the coolest female on the planet. Partly for being Nigel Adams's offspring, partly because her legs are as long as a racehorse's. I kick his mattress again. "Tell me! Who was on the phone?"

"Some guy."

"Some guy who?"

He gets up and pushes me toward the door, tearing another Nigel poster on the way. We struggle in the doorway and I slip on the wooden floor, lose my stance just long enough for him to slam the door with me on the outside. "Some guy you have a total crush on," he hollers through the wood.

"Who?"

"Do you really need this information, Mandrea?"

"Yes!"

He sighs dramatically. "Promise not to tell about today?"

"I promise!"

"All right. It was Will Sherwood. Happy now?"

I lean against the wall and hug myself, smiling so hard it hurts.

Yes. I'm happy now.

chapter 3

I drop the attendance for my Spanish class into a wire basket in the office during second period. All the three secretaries can talk about is Michaela's parents' accident. The whole room is all "Can you believe the driver just took off?" and "The papers don't say how the little girl is." I lean against the counter and fuss with my shoe for a bit, just in case these ladies reveal more than Mom told me.

"They're setting up checkpoints again today, you know," says Mrs. Chalmers, the one with pictures of her wedding all over her desk. "I saw two on my way to work this morning. Pulling over every dark SUV that passes by, looking for a damaged front end."

So no one has stepped forward to claim responsibility. No real surprise. I mean, the kind of person who runs over a family and takes off is probably not the kind of person who signs up for punishment twenty-four hours later.

"Where's this?" asks Angie, the younger, chubbier secretary, who, as long as I've known her, has pronounced library as *liberry*. "Over by Disneyland?"

"Nope," says Mrs. Chalmers. "All over Orange County. Random places. Because who knows where the driver lives."

"Not sure what it'll accomplish now," says Naseem, the little one with the tidy desk over by the window. "It's been all over the news. I'm sure the driver's hidden his truck until the thing blows over."

"It's like that other time," I hear myself saying. "When that boy was killed. Tyler Glass."

Mrs. Chalmers looks up, shakes her head. "Wasn't that just terrible? Poor kid, just getting out of the hospital in time for Christmas, then killed getting into his car just across the street . . ."

"And in front of his parents," says Angie. "That was what got me. The papers are saying it could be the same person. Which is exactly what I was thinking."

"Nearly a year later and that case isn't solved. Unbelievable." Mrs. Chalmers crosses the room and scoops up all the attendance folders, presses them against her chest and looks at Naseem. "I'd love some chow mein from China Gardens for lunch. What do you say?"

"Sounds good. I'll drive this time; you drove yesterday."

I back toward the door, a bit stunned by the quick change of subject. This is what it would be like to be someone other than me—I could hear terrible news and then wonder what to have for lunch. That's how detached you can be when a little girl isn't cuddling a stuffed dog in the corner of your bedroom.

Just as I pass the English building, I spy none other than Brayden and his band of goons cutting class again. They're hiding between some bushes, leaning against the wall of the English building as if no one can see them. Here's the thing about Brayden's friends—they're going nowhere. One of them, Dillon, is repeating ninth grade for the third time. And another, Tomas, was caught breaking and entering an empty house over in Placentia. The idiot set fire to the carpet in the living room and claimed he did it to keep warm. To stay alive. The judge felt sorry for him because his parents were going through a messy split. But come on—the kid lives up on Diamond Ridge. No one is dying of cold in that family. Especially not in Orange County.

I walk over to them, pick up a pebble and flick it at Brayden. "Dude. You're fifteen minutes late for English."

Dillon and the short one, Ace, shove Brayden around and laugh.

"We have a substitute," Bray says, pushing his friends off. "No one's in there. We don't have to go."

"Should I mention this to Lise, Bray?"

"No!"

"Then get going." I wait and watch while Brayden, with great reluctance, says goodbye to his doofus friends and heads for the door. He moons me real quick before disappearing inside. Once I'm sure he's not waiting for me to leave so he can slip out again, I head back to class.

I hear an acoustic guitar being strummed in the music room of the Arts & Language building. So soft you can barely hear it. And if you're thinking there's nothing weird about a guitar being played in a music room, think again. The music teacher, Mr. Buchanan, is this really old grizzled guy who wears T-shirts with the sleeves cut off to show the muscles he might once have had. And if he ever really was a tough guy, all that's left now is that he teaches self-defense at the retirement center on Thursday nights and is seriously manic about his instruments. No one is allowed in his classroom when he's not there unless they feel like having, as he says in his croaky, cigar-butt voice, their "ass mown like grass."

For a while, it became a school-wide goal to make Buchanan mow someone's ass. Kids made plans to, say, bang their trumpets on the hard floor one morning to completely flatten them. Once someone stuffed part of a bagel down the neck of a trombone, so Mr. Buchanan had to dig it out with a pen. The ass-mowing never happened, but only because Mr. Buchanan didn't know who did what.

So now he has a rule: no one enters his room when he's not there. No exceptions. And I just saw Mr. B. in the office, trying to convince Principal McCluskey to order some kind of special mouthpieces for the clarinets, which means he's not in his room. But he will be any second.

Curious to see who the risk-taker is, I decide to travel the scenic route back to Spanish via the second floor. The door is wide open and there he is, sitting in the middle of the room with his back to me. I don't need to see his face to recognize that shaggy brown hair. It's Will.

Very quietly, he starts to sing.

I can't help it; I slip into the room. He has a great voice, all raspy and soft, and though he's singing about a girl, it isn't sappy or boy-band in any way. It is sweet and simple and makes me melt.

Once, in seventh-grade science class, Will and I were assigned a project. We, along with two or three other kids I can't remember, were to plan an eco-friendly neighborhood and sketch it out on paper. One day after school we worked at his house, because his father is an architect and he has this huge drafting table we could use. It was cool being in Will's home, seeing his room with its walls covered in cork panels. He has this huge bulldog, Mack, with a face mashed in like a rotten apple. Truly the ugliest dog ever born. And while we were taking a break to eat pizza and play video games, Will started goofing around with the dog and singing to it—that old song "You Are So Beautiful." Only Will hammed it up in this funny, screechy voice. It was adorable and beyond.

Don't ask me why I start thinking about that right now. I just do.

Will has to get out of here. Buchanan will be back any second. I lean back against the wall and accidentally hit the light switch. Right away the lights go out. The music stops. Will spins around in the semi-darkness and I do something very dangerous in my nervous state. I start to speak.

"Sorry . . . I was just passing by and, well, I heard you, and Mr. Buchanan was just in the office but he'll be back, like, any second and I think you should go . . . like really fast. He was just finishing up with McCluskey, and if he sees you, he'll—"

"Andrea," Will says, standing up and turning around. "I was working on an assignment."

"But Mr. B's going to find out."

"I'm almost done. Just wanted to practice the chorus."

My cheeks flush hot. "The chorus. The chorus was, like, perfect. It was slow and fast, and so sad but so happy, you know?" I'm painfully aware I am making him hate me with my inane babbling. It's a curse: when I get anxious, a massive amount of words come tumbling out of my mouth. And not just any words. Empty words that come out incomplete because they lack important things like thoughts. There is only one way to stop the leak. Exit, and fast. I tilt my head and move toward the hallway. "Was that . . . wait, did someone call me?"

"Listen, Andrea, there's something I want to ask you."

"Yes?"

He blushes and kicks at something that doesn't exist on the floor. He sets the guitar down, then glances up at me. He's never looked so cute. Never. It might be the sunburned freckles across his nose or the not-quite-squareness of his teeth or that impossibly deep dimple on his left cheek. Or the faded-

Levi's blue of his eyes. I bite down on the side of my tongue to keep it from leaping into action again. "Yesterday," he says, picking up the guitar again and slinging the strap over his shoulder, positioning the instrument against his back. He pauses. "Back when you and Joules were in your car."

"My mother's car. That's not *my* station wagon. I would never, you know, get a station wagon."

"Okay." He laughs. "Your mother's car."

I wait for him to continue but he doesn't. Instead, he gets all hunched and sheepish.

My insides heat up and I twist my body from side to side to keep from smiling too wide. "So, you were saying?"

"I was just wondering. I mean, I showed up kind of after the fact, but still. I saw you there in the car, in that cute red shirt, and it just hit me . . ." He stops talking and stares at me intently. So intently I start to blush.

What just hit you? I want to scream. *There I was in that cute red shirt and . . . what?*

There's a noise in the hall. I turn to find Joules right behind me, standing there in my white shirt from yesterday. She holds up a hand and waggles her fingers hello.

Of course. Will wasn't staring intently at me; he was looking at Joules Adams.

She sashays into the room and slides herself beneath Will's arm to rest her head on his shoulder. "Look at the two of you in here all by your lonesome. Should I be jealous?"

No! Joules Adams cannot be here right now. This is the single most interesting moment of my life so far—here I am, alone with Will Sherwood, waiting for him to ask me who knows what kind of question—and the Lucky One walks in and takes it from me.

"No," I say. "I was just, he was just . . ."

No one's listening. Joules is walking her fingers up Will's T-shirt and he's laughing, burying his face in her messy hair. An arrow could penetrate my forehead right now; I could drop to the floor and lie here in a pool of my own blood, the person who shot the arrow could burst in, slip on the blood and land on the floor beside me, and no one would notice. The world around these two has become that invisible.

They face each other now, and Joules rises up onto her tiptoes, rubs her nose against his. He pulls her closer.

It's wrong to look. They're too intimate, completely lost in each other.

But I can't move away. I'm stunned by the cruelty of nature. Think about it. Mice being swallowed whole by snakes? Cruel. Hurricane winds felling trees that have been growing for hundreds of years? Cruel. Me being born Andrea Birch and her being born Joules Adams? Cruel. And then for nature to dangle a creature like Will in front of me and have him openly adore the girl I am not?

Deeply cruel.

They poke at each other jokingly a bit, then he runs his hands up through the base of her hair, leans down and kisses her.

The kiss is gentle at first, his lips barely touch hers. I should look away but I can't. She reaches up for more, but he pulls back, making her wait. It's only once she allows him to lead that he moves into the kiss with more force, searching her mouth like he wouldn't mind swallowing her whole.

It's wrong that I watch. I know it. But I can't move.

Will's guitar strings collide with a desk and reverberations of musical notes strum without any rhythm. Thrum. Thrum Thrum. Thrum.

Joules liquefies—who wouldn't? It's the most perfect kiss I've ever seen, far more exciting than I will ever experience in my Andrea Birch existence. I close

63

my eyes and imagine my lips are touching Will's. That it's my back his fingers are caressing. My life his is entwined with.

The sound of shuffling. I open my eyes to find Joules and Will heading outside, and right away I'm embarrassed. Here I am, the dorky third wheel, watching them kiss, then standing there with my eyes shut as they exit. Unwilling to face either of them out in the hall, I count to ten before starting through the doorway.

Bad idea. Mr. Buchanan walks right into me on his way into the room, and he looks none too pleased. "Andrea Birch, you know the rules about my room. Report to detention after school."

chapter 4

If my mother looked upset after yesterday's detention, she looks furious after today's. As I walk across
the crispy lawn Dad tries so hard to make green—can
it not rain just once a week, for his sake?—I feel her
eyes boring into my soul.

"Honestly, Andrea. I don't know what is happening here. Is this some sort of passive-aggressive way
of saying you're not willing to help out with the kids?
Because if it is, quite frankly, I'm hurt. Not only is it
self-destructive but it's insulting. I thought I raised you
to be open with me."

I can hear Kaylee or Kaia, or both, playing in
the background. I step up onto the porch and try to
decide whether it's better to look straight at Mom or
avert my eyes in submission. In the interests of not
looking shifty, I go with the straightforward glance.

"And don't give me that look, young lady. Mr.

Buchanan tells me you were in a room you'd been strictly forbidden to enter. When you were supposed to be in Spanish."

"I'm not."

"You're not what?"

"Trying to be passive aggressive. It's not a way to get out of helping with the kids. I swear, this is all just circumstantial."

She sighs, exasperated, and crosses her arms. "Honestly, I find it very hard to understand how, after sixteen years of not having detentions, you find yourself with two in two days."

"I swear."

"The situations we find ourselves in don't just happen, Andrea. We create them. Just like we create our lives. I didn't just wake up to this life with all you kids and call it circumstance. I manufactured this family of ours."

"Yeah. I know."

"I don't like your tone!"

"What? No tone! I just meant—"

"You know, after I got the call from the school today, for the first time ever, I toyed with the idea of bringing in a mother's helper. I did. And I'll tell you something, it pains me that I feel I can't count on you. It really does."

I decide to change the subject. "Has Michaela spoken yet?"

"Maybe if I'd been able to work with her a bit. But the twins were wild today. And it's quite possible one of them swallowed Play-Doh."

Kaia and Kaylee toddle up behind her, all sweaty white hair and fat pink cheeks and brown eyes the size of CDs, both cute as anything, but Kaylee is whining. She tugs on Mom's pant leg. "Up?"

Mom continues. "If trouble is not what you want at school—or at home—then do something about your behavior. If you ask me, it is twice as hard to get in trouble at school as it is to just put your head down and get to work."

"You don't understand. The first time it was Joules and the second time it was Will."

"Up?"

"Andrea. Worse than getting yourself in trouble is pointing your finger at someone else."

"Up. Up?"

"I am not pointing my finger at anyone . . ." I pause to consider this. "Okay, maybe I am, but I'm not kidding when I say . . ."

Kaylee tugs harder on Mom's pant leg, then bends over to throw up blue Play-Doh on the rug by the front door. Right away she starts to wail. Now Mom picks her up. "Well, I guess we know which one of you ate the modeling clay, don't we? What's the matter, sweetness? Your tummy hurt?" Kaylee nods and tucks her delicious chin—as small and red as a strawberry—into Mom's neck.

Mom looks at me. "See what I mean? I don't blame Kaylee for vomiting on the rug. I blame myself for turning away while she was playing with the Play-Doh. I manufactured this mess. Do you see the difference?"

"Of course."

"Good." She blows her bangs off her forehead. "So what do you say? Want to clean up Kaylee or the rug?"

About three hundred and thirty days. Seven thousand, nine hundred and twenty hours. Four hundred and seventy-five thousand, two hundred seconds. That's when I'll be in my cozy, Play-Doh–free dorm room at Stanford.

"Andrea? Kaylee or the rug?"

I toss my backpack and hold out my arms. "Kaylee."

But when Mom tries to hand her over to me, Kaylee turns away and clings more tightly to Mom, wailing even louder. Mom pats her head. "Okay,

okay, nothing to cry about. You can stay with Lise."

Now Kaylee's bright little eyes look toward me. I tug on her chubby foot. "Does that mean I have to clean up the yuck? Huh, Kaylee? Are you making me clean up the yuck?"

Kaylee smiles and starts to kick, nod her head yes.

"Gross!" I say, feigning disgust. "I have to touch that blue stuff?"

Kaylee squeals, "Yes! Drea do it!"

I tickle her exposed belly now. "You want Drea to do something so yucky? You're a little bum-bum, that's what you are."

Kaylee tries to tickle me back, but in leaning forward, she's sick again; this time liquid Play-Doh spurts all over my shirt. Her face burns red and she cries as Mom rushes her down the hall to the bathroom before it happens again. "Don't forget to soak the mat in vinegar after you clean it up, Andrea," Mom calls back to me. "That way it won't smell."

Puke clean-up. That, apparently, is the life I've manufactured. Along with not being born Joules Adams.

Mom's voice. "And make sure Kaia doesn't get into it!"

Too late. Kaia has seated herself cross-legged in front of the pile of slop and has already driven a car through it. On the floor now, I pull off my already ruined shirt, take the car from her, and, sitting in the hallway in my bra, I clean the toy with my top. "Uh-oh. We got Hot Wheels in the vomit."

Kaia pokes at my abdomen and laughs. "Drea belly buttin."

"You're a belly buttin, Kai-Kai."

She chortles in delight as I head into the kitchen for rags and water. "No. Drea belly buttin!"

Just then Brayden thunders in with two of his friends. They take one look at me returning with a bucket in my white sports bra—fraying at the edges and rendered dingy gray from an unfortunate incident involving hot water and a black sock—and nearly fall over shouting and laughing as I hide behind the bucket. Brayden squeals, "Ugh, the horror. You've burned out my eyes!"

I threaten to swat him with a sopping rag and he stumbles toward the back room with Tomas and Ace in tow, all bumping into each other and the walls as if blinded.

"Morons," I mutter.

Kaia stands up and waddles after them. She claps her fingers on and off her eyes as she goes. "Owowow, burned a eyes too!"

With a great sigh, I plunge the rag into the bucket and think about cleaning up the rug. I try not to think about destiny, what's on my shirt, what Brayden will say about my raggedy bra tomorrow at school and, most of all, where Joules Adams's lips are right this very moment.

•

Later that night, once the twins are tucked in and Mom is giving Michaela a bubble bath, I lie on my bed and consider what, exactly, is lacking in my mother. I get that she wants to give back to foster kids, but why so many? Why so extreme? And was having *one* natural child part of her grand scheme—so this fortunate person could grow up and eventually fill the role of unhired and unpaid help? My mother should consider herself lucky I was a girl. Imagine if Brayden had been her natural child. He'd have been no help whatsoever. She'd never have been able to take in so many kids. She'd have had to fulfill her dream with beings less demanding than human children. Guinea pigs, maybe. Or Sea Monkeys.

There's a knock on my door. At least someone in this house still honors rules. I tell whoever it is to come on in. It's Cici and Sam, dressed in runners, shorts, baggy T-shirts and sneakers.

"She's making me jog," Cici whines, pointing her thumb at Sam. "Wanna come make fun of her?"

Sam slaps her thighs. "I want to have a tighter butt by next spring. This jiggle is unacceptable. I look like J. Lo."

Cici starts laughing. "J. Lo would die of insult."

"You're not fat or jiggly, Sam," I say.

"I am. It's okay, I can take it." She tugs at her shorts and sucks in her belly. "But by April, watch out!"

"Maybe if you ate one less bag of Doritos each day, I wouldn't have to go through the torture of running." Cici looks at me. "Please come, Andrea. It'll be so terrible."

I grin. "As tempting as that sounds, I'm pretty sure Mom would interpret the horribleness as fun and insist I return to jail."

They leave.

Once they're gone, I figure it can't hurt to earn a few brownie points with Mom. I cross over to Michaela's side of the room and straighten her pillow and covers. I set the stuffed dog under the sheets as if he's waiting for her. Then I take her pajamas into the bathroom and ask Mom if she'd like any help.

Mom looks tired. She's on her knees, bent over the tub, where Michaela sits staring at the wall while her neck gets washed. The girl doesn't acknowledge me as I enter, nor does she acknowledge that anyone is scrubbing her neck. It's as if she's blind and deaf. Mute, too. She reminds me of Helen Keller, closed. In her own private world, not allowing anyone else in. Not that I blame her.

"Did the flowered pants lady say if Michaela was always like this? Quiet, I mean," I ask.

Mom looks up. "Who's the flowered pants lady?"

"You know, the one from Child Services."

"Huh. I never noticed her pants."

"They're kinda hard to miss."

"Anyway, no one at CS knows anything about her life before . . . you know."

"How are her parents?"

Mom shakes her head as if to say "Not in front of Michaela."

I hold out Michaela's folded pajamas, hoping to soften Mom's edge. "Do you want me to dress her?"

"I think we should disrupt her routine as little as possible. Just leave the pajamas on the counter and I'll get her ready."

I do as she says but stay in the room to help with

brushing her teeth—I'm in charge of the young ones' teeth. Always have been, always will be.

Mom gets Michaela to stand up, then wraps her toothpick body in a towel. As she pats the child down, she turns to face me. "Is there something else?"

"What? No, I was just waiting to do her teeth . . ."

Michaela starts to drop back into the water, threatening to soak the end of the towel. Mom grabs for the end and scoops Michaela back to standing, sloshing water all over the floor. I drop down with another towel to sop up the mess but Mom shoos me away. "All right. This bathroom is too small for three of us. Please go get Michaela's bed ready for her."

"I did," I mumble as I leave the room. "I did get her bed ready."

The phone rings from the hall table. I rush to pick it up before the ringing wakes the twins. "Hello?"

"Andrea?" It's a male voice. Dare I hope? "It's Will."

I press the phone against my chest and try to breathe. Will. Calling me again. It's weird how different his voice sounds—if anything he seems closer than if we were standing side by side. The intimacy of it makes it hard to breathe. I untangle the long cord and race with the phone to my room so as to have a bit of privacy before Mom brings Michaela in to tuck her under the covers. Quietly, I shut my door and dive onto the bed. "Hey. Hi."

"Hey. I hear you got into trouble today. Feels like my fault."

"No. I mean, yes, I did get into trouble, but I don't blame you. Not at all. I mean, yes, it was because of you I went into the room, but how could you know what I would do? You were just minding your own business like I should have done. I should have ignored the sound of the guitar and continued on my way to Spanish instead of spying on people on the second floor. Not that I was spying. It's just that I'd seen Mr. Buchanan a few minutes before, back in the—"

"Andrea?"

Of course. I'm babbling. Stupid me. "Yes?"

"Remember I said I wanted to ask you something?"

"Yes. But Joules came in and then, well. Then things kind of got uncomfortable. Not for you, obviously. For me." I lie back against the pillow and touch the spot where I'd like his head to be. Close enough that our hair gets tangled.

He pauses. "Yes. I was just going to ask if, yesterday, when you were in the car and all that . . . ."

75

He's silent. I squish the pillow to make a groove for his head. "Yes? When I was in the car?"

More silence.

"Will? Will?"

The phone's gone dead. And the timing could not be worse. He was right there, about to say something really important. Important enough to call me about. *Twice.* Just as I'm climbing off my bed to try another phone, Mom walks in with the other end of the phone cord in her hand.

"Why is the phone in here?"

"You unplugged it?" I squeak in horror.

"I tripped over the cord, then came looking for it."

"Please can we plug it back in? Will was in mid-sentence. He'll think I hung up on him."

She narrows her eyes and ushers the pajama-ed Michaela onto the cot. "Isn't that the boy you mentioned earlier? Will?"

"Yes."

"He's the one you're acting up for?"

"No! He has nothing to do with any of this. Please let me call him back. He'll hate me for hanging up."

"I need to make a phone call. You'll see him at school tomorrow. But, seriously, you should think long and hard about this boy. I'm not sure he's a great influence on you."

"Mom, please. I need to just call him real quick. Then I'll think long and hard while you make your phone call."

"Sorry. I have to make my call before eight. It's to Child Services, so I'll be a while."

"But Mom . . ."

Michaela clutches her dog and starts to whimper again. Mom sits down beside her and pets her forehead. "Andrea, please. You'll see him at school tomorrow."

She turns off the lamp beside the cot and, as impossible at it seems, Michaela's breathing slows to a steady rhythm. One thing is certain, she falls asleep fast and hard. Mom motions for me to turn on my bedside lamp, which I do, then she flicks off the overhead light and comes to sit on the foot of my bed, I'm sure, to have a mother–daughter talk. To tell me she understands how crazy life in high school can get and knows what it's like to love a boy. Maybe even to reconsider the phone call with Will.

"Mom, please let me explain about Will. It's not what you think . . ."

"I can't take in any more today, Andrea. I have a headache; I'm exhausted. All the little ones are in bed and I'm done with anyone under the age of twenty."

She tosses something onto my lap—the bedazzled

77

rubber gloves from Gran—then stands up and yawns. "Clean up the kitchen before you turn in, will you, please, honey? And make sure to scrub the spaghetti pot with an SOS pad. The sauce burned the bottom and it's all caked on." She closes the door behind her.

On the floor, where Mom's feet just were, is a balled-up Kleenex she probably used to wipe someone's runny nose. As I stare at the crumpled tissue, I swear to God, I start to hate that little wad, the way it's tilted up to look at me. Its crevices resemble a horrible face with slitty eyes—and it appears to be mocking me.

I slip my hands into the gloves and pick up the snotty tissue. Then I take it over to the trash can and rip it up into tiny snotty little pieces. When there's nothing left that is large enough to rip, I drop it into the garbage and push it down with my foot.

I pace around the room like a caged I-don't-know-what. Animal. I'd say leopard but I'm probably more like one of those monkeys who lopes along sideways as if one of his legs is turned the wrong way. Doesn't matter. The point is, I can't take my life any more.

Standing in the glow from my lamp, I stare down at the gloves. This is it, then? This is what I was meant for? To be someone's slave girl, to be ordinary, to never have my needs met? Furious at my mother, I watch the way the jewels flash and spark in the light.

Then something strange happens. And it could very well be my anger shooting out through my hands, or the ugly color of my destiny winking at me, but for a second, a half-second even, all the gemstones flash green. And then it ends. Back to plain old, plain old.

Kind of like me.

I can't do dishes right now. I can't. I'd throw the plates on the floor and roll around on them just to feel the china pierce my skin. I feel like I'm trapped—I can't even play music in my own room. I stare at my Stanford letter for a minute, but not even Mortimer Wolf can cheer me up right now.

I have to leave. Go. I have to be anywhere but here. I yank open my window and tear a few leaves off the rosebush growing over the sill. Even through the gloves, a thorn pricks me. Then, with a quick glance to make sure Michaela is still asleep, I climb outside, drop quietly onto the grass and start to run.

I don't know how long. I don't know how hard. I don't even know where I am. Past my school, I know that much. Past Laura Belanger's house near the old theater. Past the little store where my Mom once bought white Birkenstocks, which kills me a bit. I mean, who buys white Birkenstocks? Mom just isn't into making a personal statement with her outer self. If anything, the appalling state of her clothing and sandals and her unpolished toenails *is* her statement. As if she's saying, "Here I am. I dare you to judge me." The trouble is, jerks like the sales guy that day do judge her. I could tell from the way he packed the white sandals in the box and smiled—more to himself than to her—and said, "Well. You know what works best for you."

Jerk.

At some point it begins to rain. Hard. My skin is wet beneath my shirt and water trickles into the gloves to pool at my fingertips in a way I can only describe as disgusting. The train underpass looms ahead in the darkness and I start to run for cover beneath the bridge, but my waterlogged shoes make for a slippery climb up the embankment. I stumble a few times, scraping my knees, before setting myself in the dirt and listening to the drum of rain on the steel girders overhead, and the sound of the odd car tearing through puddles down below.

It makes no sense, this life. I mean, who decides which kid gets sent into which family, which house, which body? Who did I wrong to wind up assistant caregiver to so many needy kids? And what about Joules? Was there a lineup for her position in life?

Then you have the self-centered ones who don't waste a minute of their time worrying about what the rest are going through because none of it is happening to them. About 90 percent of my school is made up of these morons.

You know what I think? Morons like these, whether they're rich or poor, beautiful or toadish, *they're* the lucky ones. They get to float through life under the illusion that the world is a reasonable place.

Me? No luck at all.

I look down at the road below, watching cars splash through the puddles. A dark SUV zooms past, but it's hard to tell if it's black or navy blue. Or if it has a dented front end. I wonder if the driver's been stopped at one of the roadblocks and how guilt-inducing it would be right now to be the owner of a black sport utility vehicle. You'd feel like the eyes of the entire county were upon you.

The rain intensifies, battering the metal bridge overhead like zillions of tiny hammers, forcing a small car to pull under the bridge and stop. A driver hoping to wait out the barrage. I watch as a girl gets out the passenger side. She leaves her door open and trots to the back of the car to dig for something in the trunk.

Music from inside the car echoes off the bridge structure and my stomach sinks as I realize what song is playing. "Rockabye" by Nigel Adams. His latest single and the title track from his new CD. Rumor is he wrote it for his daughter. His Jujube.

I hold my sodden T-shirt away from my body and shake it, trying not to imagine Nigel singing it to her at this very moment. How easy she has it. I stare down at Gran's crazy, rain-filled African gloves and think about the stack of dishes that awaits me at home. What awaits Joules Adams tonight? A phone call from Will—one that doesn't get cut off by a mother with military rules? Or maybe she's with Will right now. Maybe they're enjoying The Kiss—Part Two.

And she called me lucky.

The ground beneath me starts to rumble as a train approaches. The sound of it roaring past overhead is violent. I clap my hands over my ears and try to ignore the grit raining down upon my head. The train is impossibly long. I need to distract myself from the roaring in my ears. Think. Think about something. Someone.

Will Sherwood.

I close my eyes and imagine the impossible.

I would give anything—*anything*—to have swapped places with Joules in that music room. To stand so close to Will I can feel his breath on my eyelashes, in my hair. I would give anything to have him lean over me and kiss me the way he kissed her.

I would give anything to switch lives with Joules Adams.

chapter 5

I wake up to the sun shining in my eyes. I've never known a morning so bright. I roll onto my stomach and bury my face in the pillow, hoping to catch a few more minutes of sleep before the twins start howling and yowling for their morning bottles. My pillow—it feels fatter than usual. Softer, too. I hoist myself up on my elbows and stare down at it. My pillowcase is black and a feather is poking through it.

I don't own a black pillowcase. Or a feather pillow.

I look up, confused. The sun doesn't normally stream in my bedroom window, either. This window must be facing east.

Which means I'm not in my room.

Which means I'm not at home, and let me tell you, there is nothing freakier than waking up in a place you didn't go to sleep in.

There is no corkboard with a Stanford letter

84

pinned to it. There's no dresser with a missing leg being held up by two encyclopedias until Mom finds time to take me shopping for a new one. And most of all, there's no army cot in the corner. No bruised and frightened child who is too traumatized to speak.

I'm in a room I've never seen in my life. It's totally amazing, with one wall covered in distressed black leather, the other walls papered in hot pink. A chandelier made of black and purple crystals hangs from the ceiling, and a black, glittery fishing net canopies the bed.

It is the weirdest, most fantastic bedroom I could ever imagine. I must be dreaming. I reach up and slap my cheeks, pull my eyes open. No, I'm very much awake. Not only that, I have a nose ring.

But what on earth am I doing here? I climb out of the bed and pull the hairy, gray Yeti covers up like Mom taught me (some habits just stay with you). Then, because I'm wearing nothing but boy shorts and a camisole—someone else's boy shorts and camisole, which weirds me out beyond belief—I reach for a piece of clothing hanging from a hook marked "ROBE." Only in place of a robe there's a long military coat, vintage, with silver buttons down the front and epaulets decorated with gold stars.

If I had to guess, I'd say I'm in the bedroom of a seriously flamboyant soldier. Or the soldier's flamboyant sister, and thanks to her he has nothing to wear while battling on the front lines.

I don't know where I am or how I got here. But it's almost 7 a.m., and if I don't get home quick, my mother is going to kill me.

Slowly, silently, I open the door and peer out into the hall, which is the exact same hall as we have only this one is paneled in wood. Come to think of it, the bedroom I woke up in is the same as mine at home. This house is the same model as ours, just so much cooler.

It's then I remember I'm in bare feet. I tug on a pair of tall rubber boots I saw on the floor and creep along the black shag carpet toward a foyer that should offer up a front door. My breath catches in my throat as I realize that the walls in the dim hall-way are covered with framed photos of none other than Nigel Adams, next to famous people like David Bowie and Mick Jagger and Cher, and the Lucky One herself, Joules.

My heart thumps so loudly I can hear it. I'm in Joules's hallway.

I'm in Joules's house.

My hand flies up to my nose. I'm in Joules's nose ring—and I don't even have a pierced nose!

I have to go. Any second now she'll come out and see me. Have me arrested, scream for her dad's security—maybe even a team of guard dogs. Though, I have to say, this does not seem like the kind of house a rocker guy with a new CD would live in. More like the lovely house the rocker guy would buy for his mother once he makes it big, so she no longer has to live in a rusty trailer.

I pass a big mirror and stop. Even out of the corner of my eye, even in a dead soldier's overcoat, something doesn't look right. I stare at myself and nearly faint.

It isn't me in the glass.

It's Joules Freaking Adams.

chapter 6

bolt through a living room darkened by closed curtains, scattered with old pizza boxes and empty beer cans, and out the front door. I'm completely disoriented. There are houses that look like mine on one side of the street, but the other side drops off to a gorgeous view. Wait—I'm on Skyline; that's where I am! It's where all the kids—well, not *all* the kids—come to park and make out until the cops shine their flashlights in the windows and tell them to get moving.

It means I'm not that far from home. Just across State College Boulevard and I'm there.

Whoever I am.

I run. In clunky boots and coat that comes to my ankles, I run all the way to Highcliffe Court, where I race along the side of the house to my ground-floor bedroom window, still open from when I snuck out last night. I poke my head—Joules's head!—inside and nearly throw up when I see myself asleep in my bed.

I climb in through the window, cross the room and shake my own shoulder. I watch, choking back vomit as I see my body turn around to face me, open its eyes and gasp.

I clamp my hand over the Andrea body's mouth and say, "Are you Joules?"

"Yes! Who the frig are you?" she says once she gets free, and I cover her mouth again. I can't afford to have Mom race in here, not until I figure out how to undo whatever has happened.

"I'm Andrea. And don't yell—we have to fix this before anyone wakes up."

She rips my hand off her—my!—face and her hands roam over my body, stopping at my chest. "Oh no," she wails. "What's going on?"

I can't help it—does that mean . . . ? Yes! Joules's magnificent breasts grace my usually unimpressive chest. I touch them a moment—through the coat they feel like oversized dinner rolls, but still, it's a sickening thrill.

"Where were you last night?" I ask. "I don't remember anything—"

"I don't get it," she wails. "What's going on? How is this possible? This isn't possible!"

"What were you doing last night?"

She ignores the question. "Ohhh, why is this happening? I want to go home. I want to be me! What did you do to me?"

"I don't know. You're me. I'm you . . ."

Joules as Andrea jumps out of bed, looks in the mirror and screams purple murder. Sure enough, about three seconds later, my mother bursts through the door.

"What on this sweet, green earth is going on in here?" She looks at me. "Who are you and what are you doing in my daughter's room?" When I don't answer, she marches over to me and motions toward the window. "You climbed in from outside?"

I grab her hands. "Mom, it's me. Andrea."

She pulls her hands away. "What are you talking about?" She turns to Joules. "Andrea, what is she talking about?"

It isn't until now that I realize what I've gone and done. My wish last night.

Sitting beneath the train.

I wished I had Joules's life.

Stupidest thing ever!

Seriously.

Oh my God.

Look what I've done!

My breath comes in ragged puffs and I try to control it before I pass out. I mean, if you think about it, I was upset last night. And not just any kind of upset—I was climbing out of my window upset, running through the rain upset, seeing crazy faces in balled-up Kleenex upset. And you've got to admit, it's at upset times like these that people do really idiotic things, right?

Right?

"It's true," I say, my voice—Joules's voice!—shaking. "I'm Andrea, Mom! You have to believe me."

"This is ridiculous."

I can't even blame her for not believing me. Who would? "I can prove it! My training bra. You said it was worn by thirteen girls other than me. You said it to that reporter. Remember?"

She glares at Joules. "Andrea, escort your friend out. Now!"

"No. Wait!" I say. "I'll think of something else . . ."

It's at this moment that I realize something about my room is different. Michaela. She's not in her cot. "Wait. Where's Michaela?"

"I've got her in my roo—" Mom stops, suspicious. "What do you know about her?"

"I told you, Mom, it's me!"

"Andrea." She turns to Joules. "You weren't to talk about Michaela to anyone. I thought you understood the importance of that."

"I'm not Andrea!" Joules wails, waving her arms toward her—my!—body.

Mom starts nodding her head real fast the way she does when she thinks she's onto some hot clue. "Are you girls high? Is that what's going on here—you're strung out on, what, on crack cocaine?"

Joules is still running her hands over my Andrea body in horror and doesn't answer. I can see Mom getting ready to call in the feds.

"No!" I squawk. "No one's high on anything. We're telling you the truth."

"Well, whatever's going on, I don't like it. It's barely seven-thirty in the morning and my daughter is entertaining a stranger dressed like a dead soldier." She eyes the coat with suspicion, as if I'm about to try to hawk stolen goods I have hanging from the lining. "Off you go, then. And I'll thank you to use the front door rather than stomp through my roses in those clunky rain boots."

I look stupidly at Joules for help, as if she might have an answer for us.

Mom stands firm. "On you go. Or I'll call the police and you can explain to *them* what you're doing here. Whatever you wish."

Wish.

Something occurs to me.

I brought all of this on. I wished for Joules's life last night, in the rain, under the bridge. So it makes sense that if I wished it into being, I can unwish it just as easily. I take Joules by the shoulder of my favorite nightgown and pull her to her feet. Into her ear, I hiss, "Throw on some sneakers and a sweatshirt and follow me. I think I know how to fix this thing."

"I heard that!" says Mom, blocking the window. "Andrea, you're not going anywhere right now . . ."

Joules throws on a hoodie and takes my Chucks in her hands. Together, we race to the front door and outside, tearing down the street as Mom—appalled by our total disregard for her orders—hurls threats in our wake.

One thing is sure. If I survive this screwup, if I ever get myself back into my body, I am so done for.

I can't run like myself. Either Joules is a smoker or her lung capacity is ridiculously small. Besides that, I've got her breasts heaving up and down and throwing me off balance. By the time we get to the bridge, I'm clear out of breath—no kidding. I stop and lean over my knees and try hard not to die.

Joules stops alongside me—the run was no problem for her—and I motion for her to follow me up the concrete embankment.

"What the hell happened?" she shrieks at the top, her head nearly hitting the underside of the bridge. "How is it possible that you're me and I'm . . ." a small sound escapes her throat, "you?"

I pull her down to sitting. "I might have made a sort of really stupid wish last night."

"You wished this?"

I shrug and run my hands through the bits of gravel by my side. "Not a real wish, no. I mean, yes, I did, but I didn't think it would actually come true. That I'd actually wake up in your room—"

"So this is all your doing! You did this to me. Us."

"Sort of."

"You wished you were me and then you slept in my bed?" She looks enraged at this. Like she might hit me. It might not be a problem taking a punch from Joules, but I've spent a lifetime lifting small children and collapsing and un-collapsing rusty strollers. Those arms she's inside of are strong.

"You slept in mine," I say. "What's the difference?"

She grimaces. "Just, nothing. I want to be me again. I want to BE ME AGAIN!"

A couple of joggers below on the sidewalk stop and look up. I pinch Joules in the arm—careful not to leave a bruise. "Just chill out, would you? All I have to do is make the wish again. Then we're both back to normal, right?"

"I don't know, idiot! All I know is you're some kind of freaklady witchperson!"

Ignoring her, I close my eyes and try to get more specific about what, exactly, happened last night. I sit taller, look at Joules. "I know! A train went overhead. When the bridge was rattling like it would fall down and crush me, that's when I made the wish."

"Seriously? Is that all it will take—a train going overhead?"

Her confidence in me might be a bit premature. It's not as if I know what I'm doing. "Yes. Definitely."

She seems convinced. Which, of course, terrifies me because I have no idea if I'm right. "Okay," she says. "When does the train come?"

95

"I don't know, it's not like I have a schedule! But soon. It's almost rush hour, so one has to come soon."

"Good. We'll wait." She's calmer now. "Did you brush my teeth this morning? You have to floss twice a day. It's what I do." She almost smiles. "I do have a boyfriend to consider. I never know when I might get kissed." Suddenly she appears worried. "Wait. Will didn't come over last night, did he? You haven't, like, done anything with him, have you?"

As if. I haven't done anything with any boy in my entire life. "I wish."

"Wait," she says, sitting forward. "*I* was with Will."

"What?"

"You wanted to know where I was around ten o'clock. We were in his car. And do you want to know something weird?"

"Not really."

"We were talking about you."

This is hardly believable. "No way."

"He asked me something about you, I don't remember what. And I kind of flipped out on him."

"Over me?"

She shrugs. "I get all jealous over crazy stuff. Stuff that doesn't have a hope in hell of happening."

"Like Will Sherwood actually liking Andrea Birch," I say, not so much to her as to myself because it makes me realize I am not the only one who sees me as a loser no one would ever look at twice. People like Joules see me that way too. I stare at the face I've had since birth and feel pretty damned sorry for Joules for being stuck inside it. She's kind of selfish but she doesn't really deserve to be me, for even a second.

"Wait! I just remembered . . ." A look of horror washes over her face—which has paled to near-white—and she claps a hand to her mouth. "Oh God."

"What?"

She forces the hand into her lap and shakes her head. "No. It's nothing. Forget it."

I'm about to press her further but just then the ground begins to rumble. I grab her forearms and she pulls away. As the train draws nearer, I shout, "Hold on to me. Just in case. So we don't switch into someone else. Or something else."

She relents. We sit facing one another, hand in hand, and as the train thunders overhead, as grit and bits of trash swirl all around us and our hair whips in our faces, I call out, "Make a wish with me, Joules! Wish us back to normal again! NOW!"

I close my eyes and, as hard as I can, wish myself back into my body.

Grit hits my face and the roar up above is deafening. Tiny rocks patter down on top of us and sting our arms, legs, cheeks. Part of me wants to run out from under the bridge before I wind up with a concussion, but I need to stay put if I want this wish to work. I imagine my house. My bed. My closet full of lame clothes Mom picks up at The Clean Earth over on Harbor Boulevard, clothes I would love to pull on right now. All I can think of at this moment is getting back home. Getting back to Mom, Dad and the Ks. Even Brayden. I would give anything to clean toddler vomit off the rug in the front hall. To be given a list of things to buy at the pharmacy at lunch instead of trying out for a fashion show. Just, please, give me back my life.

As quickly as it started, the rumbling stops. I can hear traffic again. Birds. The clash of a garbage truck and the roar of a bus.

I open my eyes to find myself staring back. Which is absolutely not what I want to see. It means I'm still Joules and Joules is still me.

chapter 7

*O*hmygodthisisunbelievableIhateyousomuchforthis
you'retotallygoingtopay!" Joules lets herself fall
backward.

It didn't work.

The wish didn't work.

My breath comes so fast I might just pass out.
"What do we do? I don't know what else to try.
We're stuck. And we can't even go home. I mean,
we can go home to each other's houses but not *home*
home. Maybe, maybe we should go to the police. Or
a surgeon, you know, one of those guys who separates Siamese twins . . ." My hand goes to my chest
in a lame attempt to slow my heartbeat and I look
down again. "I can't believe you have boobs like this.
They totally get in the way."

"Will you shut up about my boobs? We have to
figure out what to do."

"I don't know what to do."

"You said you did! You said you could switch us back, remember? That I shouldn't panic because you had it all under control!"

I stand up, pace around and try not to throw up. "All I had was the train. That was my big idea, and clearly it didn't work." When I glance down at her, her face is pale like the bleached Wonder Bread Mom won't let us buy. "What? What is it?"

She waves her hands on either side of her face like bird wings. "Nothing. It's just that sometimes I panic. And I can't breathe." Her chest heaves up and down and she looks around as if a doctor might appear from the steel girders above our heads. "I can't breathe. I can't breathe." Her eyes are wild, fixed on me now.

"What do I do?" She'd better not say give her mouth-to-mouth. Though it wouldn't be as distasteful as it could be, since it would actually be my own mouth. Still, it's occupied by Joules. "I don't really remember CPR . . ."

"I don't know what to do. I'm panicking. Andrea, help me. I can't breathe!"

"Okay. Let's calm down." I bend over her and take her flapping hands in mine. I set a good example by taking in a slow breath and releasing it all relaxed. "Just settle down. Everything is fine, you're fine, I'm fine, right?"

"Are you freaking insane? Nothing is fine, you imbecile!"

"I'm trying to help you, Joules. Just take a few deep breaths and get a hold of yourself. Passing out is not going to help!"

She gulps in air as if drowning, makes sharp yelps with each swallow. "What do we do now? Tell me that. What? What?"

"We have no choice. We live each other's lives until we can switch back."

"*If* we can switch back. This is all based on one big fatty of an 'if.'"

"Of course we'll switch back. I'm completely sure, almost nearly certain that we can probably switch back. Totally."

She makes a face like death, but at least her cheeks have color again. "Great. That's reassuring."

"Well, what do you want from me? You think I like this?"

"You like my boobs."

"I said they were in the way—I never said I like them. Anyway, none of that matters. We have to get each other's lives straight so no one figures out what's happened."

"How do we do that?"

"I don't know—we just play the roles. At school. At home. My mom is going to expect a few things from you. Help with the dishes and the kids. Don't mix lights and darks when you do the laundry. Stuff like that. You have to be prepared or she'll know something's up."

Joules groans. "I do *not* do laundry."

"Too bad. Andrea Birch does."

"Fine, then you have to, um . . ." She looks away as she tries to come up with one negative thing about her life. "Oh God, you have to keep Will from finding out about me and Shane. Seriously."

"How's he going to find out? He thinks it was me."

"I don't know. I'm not sure he really believes it. Last night he was acting all weird."

I roll my eyes. "Last night when you were yelling at him? Of course he was weird, he was being howled at."

"No, I mean in general. I got the feeling he was maybe going to break up with me. He was all distant and stuff."

Could that be why he called me? To question me about Shane and Joules and who, exactly, was in the bushes? "He's crazy about you, Joules. I saw that kiss."

"Yeah, but later he seemed different. I don't know, maybe Shane said something. Just promise you'll keep him from dumping me."

"I'll try."

"Promise!"

"I can't promise . . ."

"*Promisepromisepromisepromisepromise!*"

Okay, this girl is hugely annoying. "Fine. I promise to try."

Just then my mother's station wagon pulls up and mom herself climbs out, sets her hands on her hips. "Andrea Jane Birch. Get yourself down here pronto."

Joules gets up. As she starts down the slope, she says, "And around my dad, just act normal. Kind of lazy, not too interested in school but keep my grades up and you work out every night at six on the elliptical in the back room. And don't forget the flossing. I'm manic about my teeth." She shoots me an aggrieved look and stomps down to the car. I watch her climb in all sulky and rude and wonder how Mom will punish her for it. Joules has no idea who she's up against. Maybe she should be in the military coat, if only for protection.

Which is when it hits me for real. Joules is in my life. I'm in hers.

And Will Sherwood is my boyfriend.

chapter 8

Joules and Nigel living in a house like mine makes no sense. Her house is in a more expensive area, Skyline, with views across Orange County—but in terms of the actual house, it's your average tract home. If it was the only one in the neighborhood, it would seem decent enough, but with dozens—maybe hundreds—that look nearly identical (including my own), it's not remotely special enough for a guy like Nigel Adams to live in. Either rock gods don't pull in as much money as people think or they don't bother to put their money into their homes.

The other thing that is strange, I realize, is that a burglar alarm didn't chime when I left earlier. Even we have an alarm—shouldn't Nigel Adams?

I slip back into their house, which is every bit as quiet as it was when I left, and creep back toward Joules's room. With any luck her father is still asleep, if he's even home at all. You never know with rock gods—maybe they go out and prowl around Hollywood for days. I haven't encountered a single sign of life in the place, and suddenly I realize I know almost nothing about Joules's existence. As in, is there an evil stepmother? A crazy aunt locked in the attic? Okay, I guess I know the house pretty well—there is no attic. Still, it would be helpful to know who else lives here, whether they're still asleep and if I can shower and get myself to school without having to see any of them at all.

It has a smell, this house. Like that awful kind of cheese fondue I once had at a restaurant—all tangy and sharp, it's as if whiskey has fermented beneath the floorboards. That odor is depressing as hell, let me tell you.

My own house, well, it's hard to say how it smells. You can't really smell your own house. You're in it all the time so your nasal membranes are dull to the scent and it's easy to assume your place smells like nothing. But it smells like something, I guarantee it. The best you can hope for is that it doesn't reek of fermented booze. No one's going to tell you if it does, so that's really all you can do. Hope.

Anyway, it's depressing how people's houses have

these smells. And the families never even know it. Not even the ones who are rock stars.

There was once this foster child who came to live with us, her name was Tracy. The cool thing about Tracy was that she was the same age as me. That had never happened before. She moved in when we were both nine. I overheard Mom say she was from an abusive situation, which might have meant one of her parents abused the other, or that they abused the kids—Tracy had a brother who got sent to another house because he was nearly eighteen and didn't need much care. Donnie. He wrote her all these letters but I never met him. Anyway, Tracy was obsessed with my dollhouse. Every day she wanted to play dollhouse, even though I thought we were getting too old for it.

Mostly we played after school. Tracy always had to pull all the hand towels out of the hall closet and spread them out on the floor. Then we had to put all the dollhouse furniture on the towels as if they were rugs. We never actually used the dollhouse at all. It made the house seem more like a castle, Tracy said. That's what we started to call it. Playing castle. Tracy only stayed a few months, then she got sent back to her folks. But I missed her. It's no fun to play castle by yourself, not when you're nearly ten. You feel like a baby. So I asked Mom one day if Tracy could visit. Mom didn't answer me. She got up from the table and started doing the dishes. It wasn't until she was putting them away in the cupboard that I could see her cheeks were wet from tears.

I've always thought I should have asked, but I just sat there like an idiot and said nothing. Sometimes you know the answer already. Sometimes silence is all you can handle in this rotten world.

What made me think of her, Tracy, in the first place were all the rugs scattered in Joules's house. Tracy would have taken one look, thought "castle" and started moving all the furniture around. For sure that's what Tracy would have done.

As I tiptoe toward the hallway that will take me back to Joules's room, I hear a man clear his throat in the kitchen. Then he calls out, "Bit of a late night, isn't it, Jujube?"

I spin around to see Nigel Adams, the man himself, made of stringy black hair and a face that looks like a pile of unfolded laundry. Each eyebrow is as thick as the tail of a frightened cat, and his eyes are ringed with the remains of last week's eyeliner. He's much bigger than I thought he'd be—seeing Nigel

Adams in a kitchen in the suburbs is like seeing a grizzly in a meerkat cage at the zoo. He's all giant limbs and hunched shoulders peeking through the holes of a T-shirt that may or may not have survived a shark attack. The Plexiglas stool beneath him doesn't look up to the job of supporting such a man, but he doesn't appear concerned as he leans against the island, sips from his coffee and flips through the *L.A. Times.*

"No," I say, entering the kitchen. It's an icy place with stainless-steel countertops that would come in handy should you wish to dissect a frog or, say, a Clydesdale. Same configuration as mine at home, but these cabinets are shiny like lacquered fingernails, and the fridge and stove appear big enough for restaurant use. A cigarette burns in a saucer beside him. I pull the dead soldier coat shut to hide my bare legs and smile sweetly. "I just popped over to a friend's house before school to ask a question. You know, about homework."

Now he looks up. Stares at me a moment, then starts laughing his head off like I've told the greatest joke on earth. "That's a good one, baby cakes," he chokes out in an English accent. Funny, I didn't realize he was British. Stupid of me, considering he's dressed in Union Jack pants in Bray's poster. When he settles down, he returns to his paper and cigarette. "You almost had me there."

I should be relieved. At least I don't have to suffer this man's wrath. But instead I'm mildly offended on behalf of Joules. Is it so uncool that she cares a tiny bit about her schoolwork?

"Croissants are ready." He nods toward the counter. "I made chocolate, your favorite."

It isn't until now that I realize I'm starving. Normally I don't eat breakfast, I can't stomach any food before eleven in the morning. Either Joules has a faster metabolism or switching bodies with another person is seriously taxing on the system. Inside a glass cake stand, atop a decorative napkin, are five or six croissants all drizzled with chocolate and icing sugar. When I lift off the lid, the room is filled with a scent that nearly brings me to my knees. And when I pick one up, it's soft and warm. I bite into it. So buttery, so sweet and light and soft. The little pastry is gastronomic perfection.

"Turned out perfect this time," he says. "The pastry rose up like air. I think I've finally nailed the butter–flour ratio."

Impossible to imagine this craggy rock star all

aproned up and sifting icing sugar atop his baking. "Seriously? You made this yourself?"

He laughs again and looks at me like I'm, well, me. "Are you mad, girlie? I make these for you nearly once a week."

I have to be more careful. Whatever Nigel does is normal—no matter how abnormal it may be—otherwise he'll start to suspect something is up. "No, I just meant that this batch is so much better than usual. Way lighter and, um, flour-ier."

"Exactly what I said."

I take another bite. "You might have a decent future after all."

This seems to satisfy him. He smirks at my bad joke and returns to his paper.

I need a glass of cold milk to go with the croissant, but where do they keep the glasses? A check of cupboard after cupboard reveals everything but, and I make a mental note to ask Joules for some sort of household map.

"Looking for something, Jujube?"

"I couldn't find my, um, my special glass. You know, that one I love . . ."

"All the glasses are the same. Don't know what you're on about."

Yes, but where are they? "Umm, Nigel?"

He looks up. "What do we say about calling me by my first name?"

"That you don't like it?"

"Got that right. You know your dad prefers the society-dictated alternative that makes him sound as old as he really is." He turns the page. "You calling me Nigel bursts the love bubble your dad lives in. And I don't like it outside the bubble. It's cold and cruel out there. No place for a sweetheart like me."

"You're weird." I smile a bit. Finally, I find the glasses. "Dad."

He looks up, alarmed, and for a moment I fear I've gotten it wrong again. But he stands, stretches and lumbers across the room. "Sorry, Missy. I forgot your coffee."

Nigel allows Joules to drink coffee? When I tried to sip from my mom's cup last summer, she snatched it away and informed me I could indulge in caffeine (from responsible farming co-ops only) when I grew my first chin hair, not a minute sooner. Not wanting to rush that process, I've actually been pretty patient.

"Thanks." I take a sip and nearly spit it out when I realize it's spiked with some sort of alcohol. I shoot him a weak smile. "Yummy."

Just then I notice the headline on the paper's front page: "No Leads in Disney Hit-and-Run."

It's about Michaela's parents. They were tourists, walking across the road on their way into Disneyland for a day of magic and fun with their child, when an SUV hit them both and took off. The photo shows the spot where it happened—a stretch of road all cordoned off with yellow police tape, where investigators are on their knees collecting evidence. Around them, everywhere, is shattered glass. All I can picture is Michaela, there on the road with her injured parents. No wonder she doesn't speak! At the side of the road is a small sunhat, obviously Michaela's, lying at the curb as if dead. No sign of the black SUV, of course.

"God, that's horrible," I feel sick as I think about Michaela hiding under the covers in my room. "That poor girl."

"What poor girl is this?" He looks up from the sports.

"From that hit-and-run yesterday. It's so awful."

He's silent a moment, then grunts. "Probably jaywalking. That's usually the case when pedestrians get hit. Usually their own fault."

I stare at him a moment. It's like the ladies in the office yesterday morning. It's like maybe every person who doesn't have the lady in the flowered pants bringing yet another damaged kid for safekeeping. To all of them, news like this is barely real. I turn back to the article. "It says to be on the lookout for a black SUV with damage to the front end and windshield."

"Only about a hundred thousand of those in California." He gets up and cracks a few eggs into a pan, then tosses in a blend of spices too pungent for a girl who has spent the night becoming someone else. He looks at the clock. "Getting late. Unless you want to wait for a super-spiced omelette, you'd better go get ready."

So Nigel Adams does care about Joules getting to school on time. Even on days he thinks she's stayed out all night. The spicy smell is so overwhelming I almost gag. "Yeah. I'll go shower." I jump up and hurry to Joules's bathroom—the same bathroom that in my house is shared by seven of us.

"Remember the rule," he calls after me. "Not too long, not too hot." As I head into Joules's room, he adds, "There are people dying in Africa!"

Okay. So he might not get too worked up about pedestrian injuries, but Nigel Adams isn't the self-centered rock star you might think he would be. He actually has a heart. I wonder what happened to his daughter's. In her completely mirrored bathroom, I see zillions of Joules's reflected back at me.

It's too much.

Everything is too much—the switch, the omelette smell, the cigarette smoke, the article, the mirrors. I lean over the chrome toilet seat and throw up my croissant.

•

Later, having showered and tried (and failed) to style Joules's hair into the messy waves she manages to create each day, I wander into her closet. It's not much bigger than my closet at home but hers is not lit up by an ugly brass fixture that looks like a nippled breast that Mom refuses to change because "you don't discard that which works just fine." Joules's closet light is a small chandelier made of zillions of spidery arms, and each one has a sweet note from Nigel clipped onto the end.

"Jujube, you're my girl. Love, Dad."

"Love of my life. Cheers, Dad."

"Coocoocachoo. Yours, Dad."

And so on.

The thought of my mother clipping notes to the light fixture in my room actually makes me laugh. My notes would be more like this:

"Andrea, bring the trash cans in from the curb. Mom."

"I hope emptying the Diaper Genie is the worst hardship you ever have to face, Andrea Birch. I sincerely do. Mom."

"You left a wet towel on the bathroom floor. How many times do I have to tell you that trapped moisture breeds mildew and mildew breeds mold? Love, Mom."

Lucky, lucky Joules.

Walking into the closet is like walking into some teeny, tiny, super-funky shop on Melrose up in L.A. You know the kind—it has some too-cool-for-you name over the door like Titanium Poodle or something equally nauseating that makes you think you're not hipster enough to go in. But if you don't, you'll regret it because the place will be full of great stuff, exactly like what I'm seeing in Joules's closet. Everything vintage: shoes, belts, hats and bags. They're all in a gorgeous tangle with mountains of jeans and tops and boots.

This isn't the closet of a pampered Rodeo Drive

princess. No Gucci bags with the price tags still on. No, these things are more like the wildly cool castoffs of the coolest people on earth. Everything appears worn, scuffed, rumpled and aged to perfection. There's even an entire shelf dedicated to tiaras tarnished with rust and irony.

No one in their right mind would crave one of the Wal-Mart hoodies from my closet back home right now. But suddenly that's all I can think about.

What have I done to my life?

•

Twenty minutes later, I realize I have no idea where to begin in putting together an outfit. The choice is overwhelming and, let's face it, this junk must be fairly underwhelmed by Joules's total lack of imagination this morning. I try on several outfits and finally settle on flat, black lace-up boots, ancient cut-off Levi's, a white T and a baggy black blazer. For fun, I top it off with a man's fedora.

When I look in the mirror expecting to be thrilled with myself, I'm disappointed.

Here's the thing about wearing someone else's clothes: it might be exciting to put them on, but once you catch a look at yourself, you get depressed. I mean, just because you look all hot donuts this minute, you know it's only a matter of time until you're back on your bed in your holey sweatpants pouring broken chips from the bottom of the Lay's bag into your mouth.

But worse—far worse—is wearing someone else's body. Because all you can do is hope and pray and trust that one day you'll be back in your own.

Besides the weirdness of it, I feel guilt. Here I am fussing with clothes while Kaia and Kaylee are probably whining for their formula. And will Joules even know how to handle sterilized bottles right so the insides don't get contaminated? Hopefully Mom was angry enough to do it herself. She probably still thinks Joules is high or something, that we were trading drugs for money beneath the bridge. Mom being mad might be best-case scenario. Joules can totally handle Mom's wrath, and it would mean the kids are safe from Joules's lack of experience. Then, once we switch back, I just work extra hard to earn back Mom's trust.

The bedroom door creaks open. Nigel, who has changed into a less holey, but not completely without holes, shirt, says, "It's time."

"I know. I'll get there before the bell rings if I run."

"You're not running anywhere, sweet pea. The journalist is here from *Vanity Fair* magazine. Don't tell me you forgot that, too?"

A journalist from *Vanity Fair*? What does he need with me—or Joules? What I need to do is get Joules's carcass to school so she and I can meet and try to figure out how on earth to make things right again. "I don't know, Nige—Dad. I have a test coming up in Biology and if I miss today there's no way I can—"

He bursts out laughing and takes me by Joules's shoulder, guiding me out of the bedroom. "You kill me today, kiddle. You really do."

Her name is Amanda Rappaport and she can't be more than five—maybe seven—years older than me and Joules. She sits on the white sofa in the living room, in her super-short skirt and her blouse buttoned about three buttons too low, and tries not to look intimidated by the wooden carving of an elk head coming out from the wall beside her. As she watches us come into the room, her face pushes itself into a face that wants to say, "Aw, look at father and daughter, aren't they sweet?" but really says, "Crap, why does his kid have to be here? *Total* waste of a push-up bra."

Over and over, she tucks red, pixie-short hair behind her ears, but the hair isn't long enough to get tucked into anything. Doesn't matter, she does it anyway. Then she stands up, holds out a French-manicured hand for me to shake, which I do. Her fake talons touch my palm. "So pleased to meet you—Julie, is it?" she says.

"Joules," I say, offended on Joules's behalf once again.

"You look just like your dad." She looks up at Nige and tucks her hair again.

"Hey, my night wasn't *that* rough," I say, which makes Nige kill himself laughing.

"When did my Jujube get so funny?" he says once he can speak. I guess Joules isn't much in the sense-of-humor department.

He motions for everyone to sit down, including the photographer, who is setting up a light box by the piano. The photographer waves his appreciation but maybe isn't allowed to do cushy things like sit down with rock stars so he keeps fussing with his lights.

"So where do we start?" Nigel asks.

More hair-tucking from Amanda. I swear, she's going to dig grooves into the sides of her head. "Well, I'm sure your father has told you, Joules, that this is a piece about your dad's absolutely incredible generosity, not only with charities in Third World countries but right here at home." She turns to Nigel, crushes her breasts together as she flicks on a recorder. "Nigel, you played an essential role in the healing of the Glass family after they lost their son, Tyler, last winter. I think it's time the public—and the media—find out who you really are."

"It was a terrible time," says Nigel, shaking his head. "Poor boy, coming out of such a long hospital stay."

The kid had been fighting an illness for months and was finally allowed to go home for Christmas. Then, at the side of the road, just before getting into the family's van, he was slammed by a car that lost control. Nothing could save the boy, not even the hospital right behind him. It stunk, that whole thing. Seriously.

Amanda makes tsk-tsk sounds as she scans her notepad for the next question. "You've really taken the Glass family under your wing. I've even heard you helped them financially."

"What can I say? I have a child myself. I can't even imagine the devastation those parents must have felt. They lived through an absolute nightmare. Still living it, as a matter of fact."

"You speak to them regularly, do you?"

Nigel smiles. "Regular enough, I suppose. The way I see it, it's small things like lending a shoulder to cry on that everyone can afford to do. In fact, I'll go one step further to say that as a society we can't afford *not* to do these things. Community really does reach farther than our own front door. It's global, or it should be. Global community is what we all need to aspire to."

Nige sits back kind of satisfied with himself and I want to rewind the entire scene. Global community. It's the kind of thing that makes me cringe. I don't like when people use crappy phrases that make them sound like they're the most generous humans on the face of the earth when what they're really trying to do is sell boxes of cereal. Still, if Nigel is forking over the cash, I suppose he has the right to say whatever he wants.

"That's wonderful, Nigel," says Amanda, staring at him. She's impressed, I can tell. The whole global community thing made her forget to tuck her hair.

"We've got some really good material already." She turns to me. "And, Joules, does it make you proud that your father is so generous?"

I actually think Nigel is a pretty generous guy and all that, I really do. But part of me wants to say no, just to see how she reacts. I don't, though, because I'm not that lousy a human being. "Yes."

"Do you think it will inspire you to reach out and make yourself an example to your peers by offering to help others less fortunate than yourself?"

Reach out? Help those less fortunate? I've been doing nothing but for the past ten years of my life. I'd love to tell her how many foster children's diapers I've changed, noses I've wiped, spills I've wiped up, but I refrain. "Definitely. Nige is a fantastic role model for me."

"And let's talk about Hungry Children. Such a fabulous organization that brings so much to the needy in Third World countries. Nigel, you've been the face of the organization for how many years now?"

He blushes. "Four. Five. Doesn't matter how long, really. Only that it's helped a few others reach out and sponsor a foster child who needs it. Plus I, personally, care for a few kids in Sierra Leone. Joules too."

Care for? I chew the inside of Joules's cheek while I contemplate this. How does paying some twenty-five bucks a month constitute "caring" for these kids? You write out a check every four weeks, then scribble a letter every Christmas telling them how your car is running and how many days of rain you've had and wishing them a happy New Year! Don't get me wrong, it's a nice thing to do, but let's not confuse who is and is not "caring" for foster children.

Amanda looks at me. "He's so humble, your dad."

"Yeah. He is. Plus he makes feathery-light chocolate croissants," I say. "That's a killer combo in a father, let me tell you."

This, of course, gets Nigel in a hoot again, even makes him slap his thigh.

"And how many foster children do you sponsor as a family?" Amanda asks.

Nigel adjusts his position on the sofa before wiping his jaw. "As a family? Honestly, I'm not sure offhand . . . Jujube has hers, I have mine, all in the same village . . . not sure what the count is just now . . ."

"That many!" Amanda grins, shaking her head and scrawling something in her notepad.

After the interview, it's time for a staged, squishy, gushy father–daughter adoration session beneath what the photographer insists are "youth-making" overhead lights. I sit beside Nigel on the piano bench while he sings his new rock ballad, "Rockabye," to me. Nothing like the "Rock-a-bye, Baby" I sing to the twins back at home. This song is edgy and dark, vague too—about a kid in despair who is saved, presumably by a father's love but it's hard to know for sure.

When all the camera flashing is done and Nigel is helping the photographer pack away his equipment, Amanda looks at me. "Wow. Joules Adams, you just might be the luckiest kid on earth. Do you know that?"

I think I need to vomit again.

chapter 9

Believe me when I say that nothing, *nothing*, has ever freaked me out like stomping across the Sunnyside High School campus to where a girl leans against a building trying to light a cigarette—and realizing that girl is myself.

I mean, there's Joules as Andrea Birch, only she's somehow managed to make my same-old same-old outfit of jeans and sweater look cool. She's rolled up the jean cuffs to expose bare calves and sneaks, and the sweater—which normally hangs limp and lifeless on me—actually slips off her shoulder, revealing the striped camisole Gran brought me back from some little town near Madrid last year. Funny, when Gran gave it to me I thought it was ridiculous. It took someone with an eye like Joules's to transform it.

Weirder still? She wears my body better, too.

Still, cooler or not cooler, Joules is me, and if I

hadn't thrown up twice already I'd throw up right now. She hasn't seen me yet, but I can bet she'll have the same reaction in about thirty seconds.

I pass by an open hallway on my way to where Joules is and I hear someone say "Joules" from my left. I look up to see Will waving me over to his locker. Will calling to *me*, actually grinning and waving for *me* to join him, is a sight that floors me almost as much as the out-of-body sensation of seeing myself with a cigarette. Naturally, I forget all about Joules and what she's doing to my lungs and hurry over to Will and his floppy brown hair.

"Hey, Juju," he says as I get close. It's funny. It's a cute and cozy nickname, but the way he says it isn't as lovey-dovey as you'd think. It's more mechanical. After he pulls a few books down from the shelf, he turns to face me. "You missed Biology."

It unglues me, having him look at me so close. Knowing these lips I'm smiling with have touched his. "Yeah. Nige—my dad—had this interview and they needed me there." For authenticity, I throw in, "You know how it gets."

"Sure." He motions toward the English building. "We need to talk. Walk you to class?"

Walk me anywhere. Walk me into a pit of fire,

127

into a cage full of silverback apes, off the edge of the planet. I won't complain. I smile at him. "Okay."

We head along a covered hallway and a group of his soccer buddies race by, pausing only to take Will by the neck and grind their knuckles lovingly into his scalp. When he rights himself, he laughs and tells them off. "Goons," he says to me.

I can't even answer him because his hair is in his eyes and it's crazy adorable. But I'm Joules, right? I can do something about it. I reach up and push it to the side, but instead of grabbing my shoulders and pulling me closer like I see him do with Joules, he uses his elbow to stop me. It's not even me he's rejecting, it's her, but still I'm hurt.

Suddenly his "we need to talk" seems a bit more ominous. I've never been broken up with because I've never had an actual boyfriend, but this feels an awful lot like I'm about to get dumped.

Which Joules will kill me for.

"The other day in the bushes . . ." he says after a bit.

"Yeah?"

"Shane's been all funny since. All angry and distant. And to be honest, he smelled of your perfume after."

"What are you saying?"

"Just what it sounds like. I want to know if it was you in the bushes with him. Because Todd and Frankie say it wasn't Andrea. They swear it was you." He wipes at his eyes, then looks away, embarrassed.

Wow. He must really love Joules. He's actually trying not to cry.

No one is in the hallway. I stop and turn to face him, hating what she's done to him, longing to do what I've wanted to do for years. Kiss him.

But I don't.

Instead, I rub his forearm. "Will. I've never been with Shane in my life. I swear to God." It's true, too. It's not even a lie.

"Seriously?"

"Seriously. I've cared about you and only you since third grade."

He squints. "Third grade? We've only known each other since fifth."

"I meant fifth! Fifth grade."

This seems to satisfy him. "I don't know. I just don't think this whole thing is working out."

"You mean you and me? You want to break up?"

He shrugs. "It's just that . . . I don't know . . ."

It's going to happen. Right here and now. I'll have

lost him for Joules in less than a day. What will she do? She could ruin my entire life. She won't see that this has been coming for a while, she'll blame me.

I have to stop it.

I reach up and loop my arms around his neck. "Will, wait. I know I've been a rotten girlfriend. It's my fault things have been off."

"Well, not *all* your fault . . ."

"No, it is. Give me one more chance, Will . . ." I whisper, moving close enough that I could kiss him.

"I don't know."

"Please." My lips graze his earlobe—which might just be the softest earlobe on earth. I am now inches from his mouth. I could finally, finally have that kiss. Even for just a second. I'll take the slighest hint of lip contact.

He takes me in his arms and pulls my body closer. Then he looks down at me and moves in, tilts his head to kiss me. Closer . . . closer . . .

Just then I am grabbed from behind and ripped away from him. With Will looking on in surprise, Joules takes me by the shoulder and yanks me away, whispering, "You little skank!"

Will comes closer and nudges me. "Hey. Can we just finish our discussion?"

I smile at him as Joules pulls me farther away. "After class, okay? I just need a minute with . . . Andrea."

He looks unsure, then wanders toward the English building. Once he's out of sight, I turn to Joules. "Why are you calling me a skank?"

"You were totally about to make out with my boyfriend!"

"I'm you, idiot! *You* were about to make out with him."

She pulls me into an empty classroom. "No kissing Will. *Everevereverevereverever!*"

"Joules. You need to know something."

She gasps, horrified. "Please tell me you haven't slept with him!"

"No. He was about to break up with you."

"I don't believe it. You've already ruined my life."

I knew I'd get blamed. The breakup didn't even happen and it's already my fault. "No, I was stopping him just then. I was reeling him back in for you. He totally knows about you and Shane. Some of the guys are talking."

"Liar."

"I swear! And anyway, I saw you smoking. That is not okay with me. Andrea Birch *does not* smoke."

131

She rolls her eyes and slouches. "Andrea Birch is a bore."

"Yeah, well, if not taking cognac in her morning coffee is a bore, you may be right. How was Michaela this morning?"

She snaps the stretchy bracelet on my arm. "That wristband is a thong. 'A' for effort, though."

I rip it off and fling it into the grass. "Did Michaela settle down? Has she spoken yet?"

"Yes and no. And why does your mom keep whispering stuff about 'Michaela's situation'? What situation?"

Mom swore me to secrecy. "I don't know."

"And what's with all the foster kids, anyway? I knew your family was big, but crap."

"It's just—"

"Your mother made me wash someone's bedding! I actually touched sheets soaked in another human's urine." She holds up her hands. "These totally need to be burned now."

"Don't even think about it."

"I always thought I wanted a bunch of siblings, but now I'm not sure I see the appeal in children. They take too much work to raise—I mean, if I could raise one in a fish tank I could see having one someday.

But the way they run around all sticky and loud—and they don't even have fur to make them cute."

I stare at her, stunned. Fish tanks? Fur? I have to figure out how to switch back before she messes up big time with one of the fosters.

"They have these foster kids in other countries. You know, the snail-mail kind. That's the way to help a needy kid. Some cash, a nice letter, and boom, you're done."

"It's a good thing you weren't part of the *Vanity Fair* interview this morning. You'd have single-handedly destroyed Nigel's public image."

"How is my dad? I miss him so much." She examines my fingernails, which she's already painted with Cici's black polish. I'm not sure she's thinking about Nigel at all.

"He is not like I thought he'd be. He's a nice guy. Even made me croissants."

Joules groans and reaches for her cigarette. "I was forced to eat granola with unpasteurized honey. A person could get salmonella poisoning from your house. I should at least be allowed to smoke."

"No! No desecrating each other's bodies. Promise?"

A twisty sort of smile crumples her face and she starts to hum quietly.

"What?" I sat. "It's only been a few hours. What could you possibly have done to my body?"

"We'd better get to English. I have to present your paper on *King Lear*. It's very good, by the way. Surprisingly insightful for a girl who wishes away her life."

"Joules! What did you do to me?"

"You have good legs, Birchie. Nice long calves, compact knees." She examines them from different angles. "Nicer than mine, I think." She points at my—her!—calves. "See? My legs are puny below the knee. It's why I always wear boots."

I look down, but don't notice much in the puny department.

"What do you like best about my body?" Joules asks.

Right away, I touch her lips and think of Will. "Your mouth, maybe, I don't know." Then I remember she's destroyed some part of my physical being. "What did you do? Tell me now or I make out with Will."

"I just made a slight improvement to your ankle." She twists her left foot to reveal the word "ANDIE."

"You had me tattooed? In the two hours since I woke you up?"

I can't feel my fingers. At all. Or my toes. And I can't breathe. I'm hyperventilating. She's ruined my leg. Ankle. Joules Freaking Adams is walking around in my body, able to ink it up with anything she wants. Wait—

"My name is Andrea, not Andie. And anyway, when did you have time to do it, and why did you have to scream it out in all-caps like that?"

"I like Andie better, and the all-caps was a typo. The tattoo artist was, like, a total loser."

"Nice. A permanent typo on my ankle." I stew about this for a moment, then reach up and detach the nose ring from Joules's—my—nose.

"No," she squawks, trying to wrestle the stud from my hand. "It's too new. The hole will grow in."

"Tough!" She pries it away from me and I snatch it back again, losing my grip. The tiny gold ball flings itself across the ground and vanishes.

"Great! It's gone. This isn't even a real tattoo. I inked it in with some drawing pen from your desk drawer."

Thank. God. "We have to have rules. No permanent changes to the other's body. Including cigarettes."

Joules says nothing. Just sulks.

"I'm serious. You want me to tell Will about what happened the other day?"

"Deal. Fine. I'm good to your body, you're good to mine. And no physical contact with my boyfriend."

"I'm not having physical contact—you are!"

"Still. Promise."

"So I'm supposed to reel him back in for you but if he tries to kiss me—you—I am supposed to say no. Isn't he going to get a bit suspicious? How is that going to fly?"

"I don't really care. Just make it happen." She glares at me. "Or else."

I wander into English with bile rising up the back of my throat once again. It's nightmarish, this whole switch. Although I have to say, returning to school is kind of soothing. This is my place. English is my subject. I'm top of the class and always have been. Mrs. Leonard loves me, and her dangly star-spangled earrings that I usually find distracting because the stars clash together when she speaks and you don't know where to look, today are as reassuring as Gran's chicken soup. Should Gran ever decide to make any and, more important, should I ever have the guts to taste it. You never know with Gran. She could swap out the bits of chicken for zebra meat because a bushman in Sierra Leone gave her a good recipe.

I plop down in my seat and try not to look at Will, who is a few seats up in the next row. He's watching me, I can feel it. Right away I'm poked in the shoulder. Kirstie Parks, with her blue streak in her black hair, makes a face at me. "Birch sits there, did you kill off all your brain cells?"

God. Is everyone so mean to Joules? I stand up and catch Will's eye. He makes a confused face, as if to ask what I'm doing back here. "Right. I wasn't thinking." Joules sits beside Will. I make my way toward the front and plop down next to him just as he leans over to dig something out of his backpack. I hold my breath and wait for him to sit up again with no idea whether my botched attempt to keep him worked, or whether he's still planning to dump me.

Mrs. Leonard closes the door and starts taking attendance and I realize Joules is missing—or, rather, I am. We walked toward class together, where on earth could she have gone? Then I look out the window to see her standing on the grass between the buildings, twirling my hair and talking to Shane.

She's acting all giggly and stupid, and actually poking Will's best friend in the chest as if she'd like to swallow him whole.

I know what she's up to. Joules is trying to reinforce her story—that it really was me in the bushes with this guy. A shocked sound escapes my mouth and Mrs. Leonard stops passing out papers to glare at me. No sign of the you're-my-favorite-student look she usually sends my way. She shoots me an aggrieved, I-don't-have-time-for-pampered-teenagers kind of stare, even as she moves closer to slap Joules's report on the desk in front of me. Joules got a 97%.

It means one of two things: Joules is a brainer or there's a signed copy of Nige's CD on the dashboard of Mrs. Leonard's Toyota Corolla.

"Nice job, Joules," she says before moving on.

Will finally turns around and looks at me. He flashes me an icy smile and turns away. It can only mean I've been set up for Mission Impossible in terms of saving this relationship.

Outside the window, Joules puts her hand—my hand—on Shane's neck and giggles. The sight of this is revolting, let me tell you. Shane is one of these guys you can see coming a mile away. Always with a lewd comment or a "when are ya gonna get busy with me?" for whichever girl happens to be nearby. Not that it's ever been me. But still. It's just as nauseating from a distance. No girl in her right mind would start up with such a player.

Except, apparently, Andrea Birch.

Joules glances up at me, then points toward Will, who's looking down at his paper. She wants him to see Andrea Birch being the indiscriminate slut she isn't.

I'm torn.

I mean, do I really want Will to see me as this trashy girl who cuts English to mess around with a boy no one in her right mind would mess with? It's insane, I know, but I still hang on to this hope that one day Will might look at me differently.

As someone who is actually dateable.

So if he sees me with Shane, will he ever see me as the right type of girl? The truth is he won't. He'll think I'm someone to stay far, far away from is what he'll think.

On the other hand, I could use this time as Joules to, um, bolster a certain girl in Will's eyes. I can work like a puppet master, toil behind the scenes to make him see all that is good and decent in Andrea Birch. And Joules, unbeknownst to her, will help me by making me look halfway decent in my dorky clothes.

Of course it would be underhanded.

And unkind.

A really crappy thing to do to her, but hey, it's a cruel world, right?

Besides, Joules is not my friend. She might know me better than anyone on earth right now, but she's never once claimed to be my friend. And then there's this. I don't have to ruin things for Joules and Will. I can still do my best to hang on to him for her. But I don't have to go out of my way to slaughter my own reputation in the meantime, do I? I mean, I'm not the one who lied, cheated.

I watch her twist herself from side to side and knock my sweater farther off her shoulder, and I try not to take offense at the fact that Shane has about zero interest in whatever this particular Andrea Birch is selling. I'm not that unappealing, am I?

Joules hunches her shoulders at me as if to ask why Will isn't looking down at her right now.

I could nudge him, motion outside, whisper something like "See? I told you it was Andrea with Shane. I told you I didn't cheat on you."

I could.

I should.

But I don't. Instead, I turn away from the window

and put up my hand to ask Mrs. Leonard a question about our next assignment.

There's no sign of Joules in the grassy area between the buildings when I bolt out of class. Which is a good thing that could be a bad thing. I'm discovering that with Joules you never know for sure. She could be on her way to Algebra to score an A+. Then again, she could be getting my navel pierced.

Later today is my interview with Mortimer Wolf. In the mess of everything that's happened, I almost forgot. Now Joules is going to show up instead of me and that's seriously going to jeopardize my future.

What I need to do is find her and coach her on exactly what to say: my whole speech about how I hope to become a better person at Stanford and how I've been doing volunteer work for Child Services in my spare time and all that. The volunteer work just happened to have been in my own house. I might even write out my resume in point form on her palm because you can't trust a girl like that to remember everything. You can't.

At the base of the stairwell is Shane. He watches

me with a grin so revolting that I consider turning around and heading back upstairs, but there are too many kids coming down behind me. At the bottom I pretend I don't notice him and let the crowd of bodies carry me along the hall toward Leighton Auditorium—not that I have any business heading there. Eventually, he catches up with me and whispers "Hey you" into my ear. Then he slips a note into my pocket.

I half smile and follow the others into the auditorium to escape him. There seems to be an anti-smoking lecture about to get going for the ninth-graders. I try to head out the side door, but the house lights dim and the presentation begins with a lousy skit composed of two niners dressed like dinosaurs pretending what made them extinct wasn't a meteor or an iceberg but a pack of Camel cigarettes.

Mr. Mansouri is blocking my exit, and when I try to explain that I wound up in here by mistake, he tells me to sit down and be quiet. I search Joules's bag for CDs but come up empty. Great, now I'm going to miss out on Joules's spare—which I'd planned to use to prep her for the interview.

After the assembly, Will is in the quad waiting for me. Or Joules. Whatever. He sits on a U-shaped cement bench with his legs crossed and watches me walk toward him. It's exhilarating, knowing he's staring at me. It's not something I've experienced before, and certainly not from Will Sherwood. When I sit down beside him, he mutters something about a new English assignment; apparently Mrs. Leonard doled out some extra-credit homework after I left. I'm mildly disappointed that it's all he has to say and have to remind myself I'm Joules. I don't want him in love with me. I want him to fall in love with Andrea.

I struggle with the zipper of Joules's bag, hoping to find something to write on. "So, do you want to eat lunch together?"

"I have soccer practice Wednesdays."

"Right. I always forget."

"If you don't have paper, you can get the assignment from me later. I have to get going."

"No." I tug on the zipper, which refuses to budge. "I'll just be a sec." Then a great idea pops into my head and I pause. "Or maybe I can get it from Joules."

"What?"

"I mean Andrea. Birch."

He looks dubious. "The two of you are good friends now?"

I shrug. "She's a great girl." When he doesn't answer, I add, "Don't you think?"

"She's nice, yeah. But you can't get the assignment from her. She wasn't in class."

I have to purse my lips together to stop myself from smiling. He noticed. Will Sherwood actually noticed that Andrea Birch was not in class. So I'm not *completely* invisible. This knowledge emboldens me. I want to know more.

"Do you know her well?"

He stares into the trees blankly, lazily. "Well enough to know she's a good student. Good person."

Yes. Yes, she is. "Do you think she's pretty?"

I've gone too far. He squints at me, suspicious, and stands up. "Aww, I'm not going down that road again. Not after the other night when you got all squirrelly."

"About what?"

"About what I said."

What he said? What did he say? The backpack isn't going to open so I fish around in my pocket for a scrap of paper. "Remind me again what you said?"

He laughs. "Yeah, right. Do you have any paper or what?"

I do. I pull a folded paper out and open it to see— too late—Shane's name scrawled across the bottom.

Will takes the note and right away his face reddens. He looks at me with disgust.

"I didn't even read it, I swear. He just stuck it in my pocket after class."

"So it's true. You and Shane."

"No," I say quickly. "It's not."

"How long, Joules? Huh? How long has it been going on?"

"I don't know. But it was stupid and it's over. It's been over for a while now . . ."

"Yeah?"

"Yes. Totally. Done."

He stands up and rubs his jaw. Then, without looking at me, he says, "Well guess what? So are we." He crumples the note and throws it on the ground, then looks across the quad to where Shane is goofing around with some other guys. He stomps toward them, pulls Shane back by one shoulder and shoves him against the locker. Then, with Shane sputtering and denying and following him, Will marches off campus.

Joules Adams is going to freak.

A few moments later, she sashays out of a hallway, plops herself down on the bench beside me and takes a bite out of an apple. "How'd it go with Will? Is everything cool now?"

I. Am. Dead.

chapter 10

There's a thing that happens to my face when I'm mad. I've never seen it before because I've never actually stood across from myself like I'm doing now, and I've never been as mad as Joules is at this particular moment. It's weird—almost like my hair gets darker. It doesn't sound possible but it's totally true. Maybe it's an optical illusion caused by my face going white or something, but right now, with Joules's anger practically bubbling out of her ears, Andrea Birch's hair is almost black.

She doesn't take her eyes off me. "You got me dumped?"

"It's not like I did anything, I swear. Shane stuffed this note in my pocket and I forgot all about it because of the smoking dinosaur skit in the auditorium. And then with Will, suddenly the note was in my hand when I needed a scrap of paper."

"Suddenly? Just like that?"

"Yes."

She crosses her arms and studies me. "Well, now you have to get him back."

"It's your thing with Shane that ended this, not me!"

"Hmm, let's see. Yesterday I was myself and everything was fine with Will. Today you're me and now I'm single."

"You guys have broken up before—how did you get him back?"

Joules thinks about it, smiles for a second, then gets all disturbed. "No way. There's no way you're going to do what I did."

"What's the difference? He thinks I'm you."

"We need to get even." She gets up and stomps away. "Come with me."

I rush along behind her. "Joules, we need to get you ready for my interview with Mortimer Wolf. It's in an hour."

"I know when it is." She marches through a breezeway, stops at my locker, and asks me to repeat my combination. When I do, she opens it and starts unloading books and jackets and food bags onto the ground.

"So can we just take a few minutes to talk about it?"

"Can you promise me you'll get Will back?"

"I can try. That's all I can do. I swear I'll try to get him back but I honestly don't know if it's possible. You really blew it with him."

"You didn't make him look out the window in English. What was that all about?"

"You want him to think I'm a slut?"

Joules seems shockingly calm.

"Seriously," I say. "I refuse to damage my own reputation."

Still, no comment from Joules.

"I mean, we will switch back eventually. I'd like to return to some sort of a life. I don't want him—or Shane—telling people I'm sleazy."

Using a piece of cardboard, she sweeps grit from the floor of the locker.

"Joules? Can we agree on that at least? That we do our best for each other?"

In total silence, she passes me some trash and motions toward the garbage can behind us. She sorts through my binders and removes old work I no longer need, then sends me to the recycling bin. Every once in a while she checks her watch, but otherwise she refuses to speak. This goes on until all the binders are placed neatly on the top shelf, and both hoodies have been shaken out and are now hanging from the two hooks beneath the shelf.

I've had enough. "We need to go someplace private, Joules."

"Falling in love with me, Birchie?"

"To talk about the interview. Please, this means everything to me. I need you to know how to answer the recruiter."

Joules checks her watch and slams the locker door shut. "Okay, I have all the time in the world now. What do you need from me? I want to be sure I help you as much as possible."

O-ka-ay. She follows me to the big tree where I once fantasized about the two of us bonding over chocolate chip cookies at lunchtime.

"Did the recruiter call to confirm the time like he said he would?"

She nods. "Yes. Before I left your house this morning."

"And?"

"He changed the time."

I stop and stare at her. "To what?"

She smiles sweetly. "2:30."

"Today?"

"Yes."

"But . . . ." Panicked, I look up at the tower clock over the auditorium. "That was half an hour ago!"

She sashays away from me, gathering her hair in her hands and tying it into a loose bun. "Exactly. Thanks for your help with my locker. Andie."

chapter 11

There sits Mortimer Wolf in the guidance office, exactly where I—or Joules—was supposed to meet him. I can see him through the little window in the door. Only it isn't me he's meeting with, it's Jennalee Waldman, his three-o'clock, who managed to stay in her own body for the interview.

Mr. Wolf looks nothing like he sounded on the phone. I don't know what I expected, it's not as if I spent any time picturing him, but I guess if you'd asked me I'd have said he was somewhere in his twenties with the kind of padded shoulders an ex-football player might have. I'd have said longish hair for a guy and a lazy smile. In other words, on the phone he sounded more like an overgrown student who either never did well enough to escape university life or didn't have the guts to try.

But he looks nothing like that. He's this tiny corn

chip of a man with a salted face, goggle glasses and bad posture. He's wearing a short-sleeved shirt with a vest and tie, and though he's maybe in his mid-thirties and should be plenty capable, he doesn't look strong enough to be able to spin in Ms. Booker's spinny chair. I don't know why I even think of it, but right away I check his left hand for a wedding ring. All his fingers are bare, which means now I'll have yet another thing to wonder about at four in the morning. Whether or not Mr. Wolf is sad. If he's ever had a girl like him. And, if he hasn't, whether his parents are upset for him. The parents being sad that their son is sad makes me equally sad. But who knows, right? He could have a really great cat or a bird who chirps "hello" when he comes home at night.

I sit on the orange chair outside the office until Jennalee walks out with the kind of satisfied smile a girl might have on her face if she just rocked the interview and is pretty certain she's headed to Stanford next fall. It's the smile I've been hoping I might have right about now. I knock on the open door.

Mr. Wolf and his bare ring finger look up. He appears confused and checks a clipboard. "Well, I can't imagine you're Greg Lund, my three-thirty."

For a second I think I should fake it. Introduce myself

as Andrea. But what if the school has slipped him our photos to prevent kids from sending in someone more well spoken? Or with fewer zits? Or better hair?

"No, I'm Joules Adams. Andrea Birch's friend."

Now he looks stern. "Ah. Miss Birch. My only no-show of the day. Of the entire month, actually."

"Yes. It's just that Andrea had a sort of family emergency. She wanted to call but this thing—it came up so fast, and so I volunteered to come over here and explain."

"I don't tend to allow students to rebook. I come to a school once and that's that."

"But if you could just make this one exception. Andrea wants to go to Stanford more than anything on earth. And she's a great student—a very serious student." I worry I've made myself sound dull now. "Who is a lot of fun! And gets involved in school things. I'm not kidding, Stanford should snap this girl up before Harvard does. Or Yale. Don't think they're not interested in her, because they are."

"I drove all the way down here from Northern California so I could see every prospective student in one swoop . . ."

"It's a beautiful drive, isn't it? The ocean, the cliffs. Lucky, lucky you."

" . . . and I'm completely booked with students at other schools."

"But are they being wooed by Harvard? You've got to think about that."

He pulls out a little date book. "I suppose I could pop by on my way down to see my parents in Chino Hills on my day off, two weeks from now. It's their anniversary." He squints up at me. "Tell your friend to call me and reschedule for that Thursday. I could see her around five o'clock."

"No need to wait for her call. She gave me permission—begged me, actually—to reschedule. Five o'clock is perfect. Better than perfect. Fantastic. I mean, really, really a good time for her. For Andrea. Andrea Birch." I nod to reinforce my words. "Really."

He stares at me, probably relieved Joules Adams isn't the one he has to interview. "Then we're all set. Please tell Miss Birch that if she doesn't show, that will be that."

I'm grinning so hard I think my face might crack. Next Thursday. Surely I'll be myself two weeks from now. I'm usually a girl who keeps her composure. Especially around recruiters for Ivy League schools. But I can't. I bolt around the desk and give Mr. Wolf a big hug. "Oh, thank you! You don't know what this means to her. And you won't regret it, I swear."

Once he adjusts his glasses, which were knocked askew in the excitement, he reaches for his clipboard and holds it to his vest as if to ward off any further unexpected, unasked-for gushes of emotion. "Well," he says, his cheeks crimson, "if that's everything, Miss Adams, I believe I have a Mr. Lund to see next."

I walk across campus, which is emptying out of kids, vaguely aware that something has changed. I'm too stoked by my triumph with Mr. Wolf right away to think what is different, but then I hear a quiet, distant rumble overhead.

Thunder.

The sky has clouded over. Gone is the endless expanse of blue bleached to white by the sun. Now the sky is bloated and swollen, all mushy-looking and dark gray. It's about to rain, and if I'd been living at home, I'd have known it. Dad would have detected the low-pressure system moving in and he'd have tracked the air masses and calculated the amount of precipitation we're about to receive. Just like he did last night, only this one Dad will be awake for.

Wait a minute. Last night.

It was raining last night.

Maybe that's the key to undoing the wish—I need a good, solid, soak-you-to-the-skin type of rainstorm. That's it!

It isn't hard to find Joules. She's standing at the edge of the student parking lot smoking with some of the stoners who hang out behind Leighton Auditorium. Which might have bothered me before I saw the sky. I march over to her and take her by the elbow, pulling her toward an archway where we can talk in private.

She yanks her arm from me and snaps, "We're done, Birch Tree. Until you get Will back for me, I'm not speaking to you. You've messed up my entire life."

"Look at the sky, Joules!"

She glances up. "Yeah? So?"

"It's going to rain. I heard thunder, it might even storm."

"Thrilling," she says, tossing her smoke onto the path and grinding it out with her heel. My heel. Then she blows smoke in my face. "I see the whole weatherman thing runs in the family. What's with your dad, anyway? I thought he was a banker. And that Brayden—do you know he actually mooned me this morning? Like I needed to see that before 10 a.m.!"

"No, you don't get it. It was pouring the night I made the wish. That was the difference. That's what we need to switch back again."

"Are you sure?"

"Am I sure? I was soaked to the skin." I pause to think for a moment. "Wait. That's it. We should both be soaked by the rain! No umbrellas. Maybe the water acted as some kind of conductor."

"There's no way I'm going to run around in the freaking rain."

I grab her shoulder, which feels so familiar I could cry. My shoulder. I want to be inside that shoulder again so bad I can barely stay upright. "You have to, Joules. If you want your life back you'll run around in the freaking rain like a freaking lunatic."

"I hate you for what you've done to me, Andie. You know that, don't you?"

"You'll love me after tonight."

A horn honks from the student drop-off loop. There, not twenty feet from us, is a green Volvo station wagon. In the back are two baby car seats. I can't see faces from this angle, but I do see chubby pink feet, one of which is missing a sock, kicking in the air.

Kaylee.

Kaia.

Between them is a yellow dress. Grasshopper legs with bandaged knees.

Michaela.

Behind the wheel is Mom, with her blondish-gray hair flopping over one eye. Of course all the windows are open, Mom rarely turns on air conditioning. Always saving the planet.

She looks tired. Frustrated. Like she could use some help. I'd give anything to get into that car right now. Tell Mom to go lie down while I prepare the Ks' afternoon bottles. Tears prick my eyes. This is all my fault. Every bit of it.

Another beep of the horn.

"Andrea, let's get a move on," Mom says, waving her arm.

Joules looks at me. "I can't take much more of this. And what's with that Michaela kid? You ask her if she wants juice and she just stares at you. Is she mute or just slow?"

I can feel my fingernails digging into my palms.

"Your mother keeps shaking her head at me when Michaela doesn't speak. Like I have a clue what to do!"

"Michaela's had a rough time. Give her a break."

"Whatever. This switching thing better work."

"It will. As soon as it starts to rain, really pour, meet me at the bridge."

"Andrea!" Mom sings. "I don't have all day."

Joules starts toward the car, dragging her feet. "I miss my life."

"I know. I'm sorry, Joules."

"You should be."

I watch her open the passenger door.

"As soon as it starts to rain, head over there."

Joules climbs in, sulking.

"And remember," I call. "No umbrellas!"

It's nearly five-thirty by the time I get back to Joules's place, and not a drop of rain has fallen. After the first rumble, I haven't heard so much as a groan of thunder. The clouds are still hovering, but way over to the west, toward the horizon, there's a crack in their armor. A single splotch of blue is peeking through the angry gray fluff. This storm cannot just vanish, not when it's the only way to get my life back.

As hard as I can, I will the blue patch to disappear, but it doesn't budge, just peers down from someplace over the ocean and mocks me.

There's an old-fashioned car in the driveway when I arrive. All shiny and black and out of a silent movie. Nigel must have a visitor. When I head inside, I find him sitting in the living room in front of a bottle of Moët champagne and two glasses. "Jujube is home," he roars like a proud lion as I walk in. "It's a spectacular Wednesday, my sweet!"

I drop my backpack on the floor and squint out the window. "Did you see the sky? I think it's going to pour."

"I've been waiting for you to get here." He stands up and starts to unwrap the wire and foil from the champagne bottle. "You and your devastatingly good-looking father are going to celebrate in high style tonight."

This does not sound good. I have plans of my own and they don't involve champagne or any sort of style, high or low. Actually, dancing in the rain beneath a filthy old bridge probably does qualify as low when it comes to style. "I kind of have plans."

"Well, cancel 'em. Because 'Rockabye' just went platinum today!"

He pops the champagne cork, which shoots across the room and whacks the painting above the fireplace, and he holds up the bottle with bubbles oozing down one side. I rush to sop them up with my sleeve before they hit the carpet and Nigel puts his arm around my shoulders. "Huh? What do you say to that, Missie J?"

Joules's dad is so happy. It's a big moment for him. Can he help it if the person he wants to celebrate with can't get her mind off the weather? I mean, here's this guy—this generous guy who practically any female on earth would kill to be with right now—celebrating what is really stupendous news. But me, I can't drum up enough emotion to care.

I work hard to make my smile appear genuine and hug him back. "You deserve it, Nige—Dad. There isn't a rocker-dad-dude on earth who deserves this more than you."

He beams at this. "So you're proud of your old father?"

"I could not be more proud of you. Seriously." I look around. "Is someone here?"

His bedroom door creaks open and none other than the journalist from *Vanity Fair* walks out, buttoning her shirt. Ah. I should have known. But the car can't be hers. I'd have noticed it in the driveway this morning.

"I guess I should head home then," she announces

as she picks up her purse and stands hopefully before him. "That is, unless you . . . ."

He shoots her a disinterested two-fingered wave and starts pouring the champagne. Instead of handing her a glass, he takes one for himself and hands the other one to me. "Thanks for everything, Amanda. I'll give you a ring." From the way he says it, it seems she might be waiting by a silent phone for a long, long time.

She's been dismissed. She nods to me, embarrassed, dejected, and slips out the front door.

I hold the champagne in my hand and say, "I'm not really feeling too champagne-ish right now."

He gathers a set of keys. "No worries. You'll feel like it when you hear what we're about to do. Did you see my new toy out front?"

"The old car?"

"That's not just an old car. It's a classic. Come see."

With a longing glance through the window at the churning sky, I follow him out the front door. And this time I take a closer look at the car. It's boxy and high-windowed and decked out with running boards and wheels that look like jogging stroller tires. It shines. It gleams. On a sunny day, I'm sure it winks at passersby.

"Model T Ford," Nigel says, setting his champagne glass on the roof. He reaches down to fiddle with something, then lifts the hinged hood cover from the side to show me the engine—the antique-y-ness of which might impress another girl, a girl who's actually seen a modern-day engine, but is totally lost on me. "A 1926 Tudor sedan."

I nod as if impressed and say the only thing I can think of. I don't know much about cars. "Wow."

"Over eighty years old. And look here." He points to a scribble on the underside of the hood. "Ford himself signed it. Henry Ford himself!" After I look, smile, he re-latches the hood and climbs inside with his champagne.

I should focus on the car. I should focus on Nigel and his moment. He deserves this much from his only daughter. I mean, let's face it. What is he going to remember when he's ninety years old and sitting on his front porch with no more *Vanity Fair* journalists to entertain him—the times Joules ignored him? No. He'll trawl through his memory and pull up a moment like this. He'll roll it around in his head and suck every bit of joy he can from it before his nurse comes outside and smacks him for sneaking another cigarette.

Just as I reach for the door handle, the sky rumbles overhead. I look up. It's nearly six o'clock now, so naturally the sky has darkened, but some of the clouds are nearly black with fury. Without question I'm about to get my storm.

Do I really want to get into the car and possibly miss my chance? I've lived in Southern California all my life and am perfectly aware that we could go weeks without a drop of rain. And what Joules and I need is a real soaker.

I lean over and look at Nigel through the window. "How long do you think we'll be? I'm just thinking of my homework."

Again, he throws back his head and laughs. "You kill me, Jujube. You really do." He turns the key and, after a cough and a sputter, the engine shifts into an amplified rattle-rattle putt-putt. This huge grin spreads across his crumply face and he sets one hand on the gearshift.

Another rumble of thunder, and I'm not sure if I imagined it but there may have just been a flash of lightning over toward Anaheim. The storm could be here any minute. Besides that, Nigel is drinking.

"In you get, sweetheart. Let's tear this town apart like only the two of us can."

I could fake a headache. Or my period. With a girl as promiscuous as Joules a father has got to feel relief every time she gets it, right? Again, I think I feel a drip of rain on my face.

"Get in!"

He looks so happy. Come on, all the guy wants is to show off his toy, celebrate his news. Am I that selfish? I mean, Fullerton is a small town, one toot through the streets and we can be back in the driveway before the storm even gets going. It'll be the gift of a lifetime for Nigel.

"What are you worried about—this?" He holds up his glass. "It's not enough to get a squirrel drunk." He revs the engine and the whole car starts to convulse.

What do I know about alcohol quantities? Still holding my champagne, I climb into the passenger seat. The magic of the moment must be getting to me because I find myself leaning across the seats and pressing a kiss to Nigel's cheek.

He looks at me, awed, overjoyed. For a second I worry he may start to cry. But he just says, "It's a good day, Jujube. A good day." Then, with two stalls and two restarts and a mighty lurch, we're off. Cruising through the darkening streets with streetlights zipping past like shooting stars, we sip champagne and sing along to "Rockabye" on the iPod Nigel has set up on the dashboard. In this fantastic old car, with champagne bubbles tickling my nose, I have to admit—it feels kind of good to be bad.

We ride along Brea Boulevard, where the boys from school sometimes have orange fights in the oil fields on Saturday nights. Along Bastunchury, where a girl I once knew used to keep her horse. Not that she ever invited me to ride it but I used to see her trotting by when I took some of the little kids to Craig Park.

And I took them to Craig Park because my neighborhood, my house, is just ahead.

To the right.

As we get closer to the bottom of the hill, I say as casually as I can, "Let's turn here. I've always liked this area."

He looks at the backs of some of the sprawling ranch bungalows, barely visible behind big drippy trees and a zig-zaggy sound barrier of a wall that travels down the steepish slope. "This area? Bloody tract homes, just like ours."

"You don't like them?"

"Like them? They all look the same."

"So, you've got money. Why don't you move?"

He shakes his head. "Better things to do with your money than custom kitchens and baths, Jujyfruit. Always remember that."

So that's the deal. He'd rather give to charity than wallow in his own wealth. I respect this guy more and more each day. The car speeds up, threatening to pass by my neighborhood. "Still!" I say quickly. "The streets in here are twisted with all these cute cul-de-sacs. It'll just take a sec and we'll loop back around here again."

He hits the blinker. "Okay. What my princess wants, my princess gets."

We turn in on Mountain Ridge Drive and wind back up the hill. My heart pounds harder as we approach Highcliffe Court. "This one," I say, pointing to the left. "Let's take a look."

He doesn't argue. Just turns left and slows the old Ford to veer around a few parked cars in front of the Hendersons'. Up ahead, there, on the right, is my house. It's only been, what, nine hours since I've been here? But it feels like years. The sight of the garage doors that once closed on my foot thumps me in the ribs. As we get close enough that I can see in through the living room window, I whisper, "Stop."

He does. "What?"

The light's on inside. I can see the foyer Mom insisted on painting powder blue because it was "calming for the kids when they first come in." The ugly painting above the sofa, the one that shows farmers so tired from their plowing that they can't straighten their spines. The tasseled pillow Brayden tried to unravel the day Michaela arrived. Impossible that it was just last night.

I'm hoping to see someone. Mom. Dad. Cici or Sam. The Ks will already be in bed, but—I can't believe I'm feeling this—but I'd love to see Bray, even. His flashy braces, his bouncy hair.

No one seems to be around. Dad's probably in the back room in his Uggs, monitoring the weather, calling out to Mom every few minutes about expected rainfall or jet streams or low-pressure systems. And he's asking the kids to shut all the windows tight and wondering aloud if all the bikes have been brought inside. It's a real treat for him when he gets to tell us all to "batten down the hatches." I feel a gush of joy for Dad. He deserves this rain more than anybody. It'll give him something to talk about for a few days.

Mom's probably at the kitchen table coaxing Bray not to give up on his Geography homework. Saying

"Be all you can be" and "You are not limited by what has come before you." Telling him he is the shaper of his own future. He's probably calling her Mom and she's probably not minding one bit.

Know what? Even I wouldn't mind it tonight.

I want to run inside and call to them. Hug them all and reach into the fridge for organic mango juice. Check the twins' breathing and see if Michaela might like my stuffed cat with the Xs for eyes tonight.

"I'll never understand builders," Nige says, bringing me out of my fantasy. He looks around at the cookie-cutter houses. "Would it kill them to change up the design a little? Give the neighborhood a bit of inter-est, less sameness? Would that cost them so much money?"

The car lurches forward and champagne splashes onto my hand. He turns the car around and I watch my house pass by. "I don't mind the sameness so much," I say quietly. "Not today."

He sips from his glass, and heads back down the hill.

As we rattle and bump our way past the rental apartments on Associated, the brown and yellow ones filled with rowdy students from Cal State Fullerton, a few raindrops start to fall. Perfect. This is perfect.

A right at the light, straight through the intersection at State College and we're weaving our way back to Skyline. I can run all the way to the bridge from the house, get myself good and soaked and finally undo this crazy wish with Joules.

I feel a gush of appreciation for the man sitting beside me. No matter what happens, it's an evening I'll never forget.

And then it happens.

Nigel doesn't turn right at the light at all. He turns left. About three seconds later, we're coasting along the on-ramp of the 91 Freeway and the rain is really getting started. A rickety windshield wiper jerks across the tiny windshield, but only on the driver's side.

"Nige—Dad. What are you doing? Shouldn't we be getting home?"

"Nah." He switches into the left lane. "I thought we'd head over to Newport. Weather's turning a bit nasty but we can have dinner at that little Italian bistro on Balboa Island. Remember it used to have candles in wicker wine bottles and those checkered tablecloths? You loved the pizza, remember?"

No. I don't remember, and I cannot possibly sit by the ocean and swallow pizza when I could be missing the perfect chance to get my life back. No matter how nice Nigel is, no matter what this means to him—I cannot do it.

"I don't know. I think we should go back. We didn't even lock the front door, it's irresponsible. We could get robbed."

He looks at me, confused. Then hoots with laughter. When he calms down he says, "No one can take what matters. All I really need is inside this car with me right now." He raises what's left of his champagne in a toast to his daughter and drinks.

Cars whiz past us, spraying water against the tinny sides of the car as we lumber along. I can actually feel rainwater splash up at the floor beneath my feet. The streetlights start to go wavy and teary in the darkness and I crack my window to help unfog the windows. It isn't until raindrops hit my arm that I realize the swimminess isn't just on the glass, it's in my eyes, which are filling up fast.

As the lights of Fullerton roll past and the little car hurtles us slowly toward the coast, which is a good half hour away in a vehicle that does normal speed, I wipe the tear that's inching down my cheek.

It won't help anyone for me to ruin Nigel's special night.

chapter 12

It's well after ten before I am able to slip out Joules's bedroom window and race toward the bridge. It's been raining hard for hours now. Nigel even made sounds about crashing in a hotel near the beach to avoid the drive home with the sticky wiper blade, but after he mentioned at dinner that he has this nightmarish distrust of cats, I managed to convince him that I might have left the back door *wide* open and that there'd been a pretty mangy cat prowling around the property in the last few weeks. Anyway, it turned out to be a good thing we came back because a bunch of people he knows started coming in carrying bottles of wine and cases of beer to celebrate "Rockabye" going platinum. And the impromptu party meant I could slip away undetected.

By the time I reach the bridge, I'm fully soaked. I mean through the bra to the skin soaked and, believe me, it is none too warm out for Southern California.

At first it looks like Joules has left. But as I get closer, I see her huddled up at the base. As I get closer still, I see she's fuming mad.

"Nice of you to finally show, you little witch," she says as I scrabble up the slope. "Do you know how long I've been sitting here? Two hours! I told your mom—she's, like, crazy bossy, by the way—I was going to take a shower, then went out your window. Your dad came driving by looking for me. I had to lie down flat. In the dark. In the gravel!"

"I had no choice."

"I have rocks in my shirt."

"Sorry."

"Please tell me you were fixing things with Will and that's the reason you left me here to rot."

"I was with your dad. 'Rockabye' went platinum, did you hear?"

She lets out a long sigh. "Shut up and make the stupid wish. I want to sleep in my own bed tonight."

I stare at her, revolted. Does she have no respect whatsoever for her father? I mean, the guy adores her. His mission in life, I'm convinced, is not to be loved by the world but to be loved by Joules. His neediness is devastatingly sad. It's not so much to ask, being loved by your own flesh and blood. It's not so much to hope for.

"It wouldn't kill you to care."

"Care about what?"

"About your dad. I just don't get you. Why you work so hard at not giving a crap about him."

She shrugs. "You've known him a day. Don't make like you're the big expert on Nigel Adams's personal life."

"Everyone can see it, Joules. Except for you."

"Shut up, Birchie. Make the freaking wish."

If Joules got drenched on the way over, she's dried off quite a bit since. Strands of hair blow across her face and she tucks them behind her ears. Soon to be my ears again.

"Go down and get soaked first." I lift my arms and watch raindrops dribble off my elbows. "I think it's the way to go. You know, water's a conductor and all."

"Yeah, for electricity, idiot. Not for body switching."

"You have a better idea?"

She picks at the ground a little, then closes her eyes and makes a pained face. "I hate you for getting me into this. And how do I know I won't be left with some hideous body part of yours—like your nose or your feet—that I'll have to get surgically removed later? I swear, if I do, you're paying for it. And how do we know this will even work? We should find some kind of expert. Maybe in L.A. or New York or something."

I swear, sometimes Joules's thought patterns astound me. "Have you ever, once in your life, heard of an expert in L.A. that specializes in body switching? This isn't a magic show, you know, where the tricks are smoke and mirrors. It's real life." I tug on her arm and motion toward the street. "It'll be fun."

"I don't want to get soaked now. I'm already freezing." But she gets up and follows me. On the sidewalk, she stops, crosses her arms and stands under the cover of the bridge.

"Come on." I wait for a lone car to pass and step out into the rain, onto the road, and twirl in a slow circle, looking up at the sky. I open my mouth and let raindrops fall onto my tongue. "Come on, Joules. It's like running under a sprinkler. Or standing in a shower."

"A shower is warm. At my house, anyway. What's with yours? It takes, like, half an hour to heat up. Plus that Samantha and Cici are always picking the lock and bursting in to look for hair clips or whatever. I don't know how you can stand living there."

"You want to shower in your bathroom tomorrow or mine?"

"Seriously, has your mother ever heard of *real* foster children? The kind you see on TV commercials? Because she'd save so much money. Plus they're from Third World countries. No one in America really needs the help."

I don't have time to shake any logic into her busted rationale. "Are you done now? Can we make the wish and get back to our lives?"

With a scowl, she steps into the rain and stands there, miserable, with her arms covering her torso.

"You have to open yourself up to it," I say, jogging in a circle, spinning and holding my arms up as I go. "Get really soaked."

Finally she does. She twirls and spins, waving her arms around as if she's flying. "I feel like an idiot."

"No one's around. Open your mouth. It feels wild."

She sticks out her tongue and starts twirling really fast in the middle of the road. I join her and we twirl around each other. Eventually, even Joules laughs and we both stagger as the dizziness sets in. She loses her balance and falls into me, knocking us both to the road, where a dip in the asphalt has created a big puddle. Without question, she's soaked now. I prepare myself to suffer her wrath—surely the falling, the puddle will be my fault as well—but Joules is giddy, drunk with it all, and she helps me to my feet.

"Okay, we're good now. Let's get up there and wish."

I follow her up. "We should still wait for a train."

"When will a train come?"

"I don't know the schedule, Joules. Soon, I hope."

We sit there throwing pebbles and shivering for a few minutes and then Joules does something I never would have expected. She shifts herself closer to me until our arms and hips are touching. She's just trying to get warm, I'm not stupid enough to think this is anything resembling closeness, but still, it feels nice. I bump my shoulder against hers.

"So what will you do first, once we've switched back?"

"I was thinking about that while I was waiting. I'm going to go straight over to Will's. His bedroom is a room built inside their garage and it has—"

"That door on the side of the house, I know."

"And you know this how?"

"We once did a group project. He showed me his room."

Her eyes narrow.

"He showed the whole group, okay?"

This seems to satisfy her. "Anyway, I'll sneak in. Tell him it's Shane he should cut out of his life, not me." She lifts her eyebrows and digs the toe of my sneaker into the dust. "After that, who knows?"

She thinks sex is going to get him back because it's worked in the past. But that was before she cheated on him.

"What about you?" she asks. "What will you do first?"

I think about the foster kids, the bottles that likely need to be sterilized, the Diaper Genie that will need emptying. "I don't know. Regular stuff."

Just then, the ground rumbles faintly. "Train!" Joules shouts. She turns toward me and sits cross-legged. "Get into position."

We join hands and stare at each other. It's a strange sensation. I'm staring at my regular face but, unlike the last time, it doesn't feel so much like the face in the mirror. I've started to get used to seeing Joules as me, seeing me as Joules in the mirror. I grasp her stronger hands and they no longer feel like my own.

The train gets close enough to hear the chug-chug of the engine. A whistle blows.

I think of my bed. The patchwork quilt Gran brought home from Ireland one year. I didn't like it at first because it was covered in these old-fashioned ladies with parasols hiding their faces—all in different colors and patterns. But tonight I want nothing more than to wrap myself in it, maybe even count the parasols, count the colors.

Finally the train roars overhead.

I shout to Joules. "Was my dad in the back room?"

"What?" Grit from above patters down on us.

"My dad. Was he watching The Weather Show tonight?"

"I don't know. He kept saying stuff about low pressure or whatever. Who cares? Make the freaking wish."

I smile. I knew he'd be babbling about low pressure. I knew it. I shift closer to Joules. "Close your eyes." I peek to make sure she does. "Turn your face up."

"There's crap raining down on me," she wails. "Rocks and sand and . . . it's disgusting!"

"Shut up and do it!" With my own face turned up, scrunching my nose as dirt falls onto my eyelids, I shout, "I wish—*we* wish to be back in our own bodies. We wish to return to our own lives."

"We wish it now!" Joules shouts. "Now!"

More grit than ever showers over us and the wind

picks up. I can feel Joules shudder through her fingers. We wait as the bridge grows quieter.

I open my eyes to see Andrea Birch staring back at me the same as before. Joules gets up on her knees, red-faced, furious. She fills her hands with gravel and sand and starts hurling it at me. It stings, way worse than the bridge grit.

"You piece of total crap!"

I reach up to shield my face. "Stop it, Joules. You're hurting me!"

"I hate you! I hate you, it's all your fault. I'm never talking to you again—ever!"

More stones. I have no choice. Andrea Birch's body is stronger than Joules's; I stand up and run through the rain, all the way back to Skyline Drive.

chapter 13

I've been cut off. Joules made it very clear. Not a big deal under normal circumstances, but as it stands, Joules is my only ticket to my family. Without her, I have no way of finding out how everyone is, no way to find out if Joules's negligence is endangering the Ks, no way to find out what's happened to Michaela, no way to wiggle my way back into my family's life, where I belong.

I get back to Skyline Drive to find the party's in full swing. There are so many cars parked along the winding hilltop road that there's barely enough room for oncoming traffic. I walk up the driveway, passing a couple of groupie types vomiting in the bushes. The scene inside is even more wild. People with cigarettes, drinks and joints fill the halls and rooms. There's an old guy with his belly protruding from a leather jacket that no longer zips. Some girls not much older than me with raccoon-smudged makeup and ripped-on-purpose fishnets. Band members, model types, even a few guys in suits with slicked-back hair and big gold rings.

They all seem to know me. I enter each room to a chorus of "Hey, it's the girl herself," or "Joules, baby," or "Jujube, come tell Uncle Chaz your troubles." I just nod and smile and pass them by. No sign of Nigel, but plenty of his friends are rifling through his liquor cabinet. I look in his room. It's occupied all right, but by three girls going through his closet, trying on his raggedy T-shirts.

I leave them to it.

After a tour of the house, it looks like he's left. Which means it's just me, the puker out front, the guy with the belly and fifty or so of our closest friends. I head into Joules's room to find a couple of guys sitting on my bed playing acoustic guitar. I turn around to leave but then think—where on earth am I going to go? Politely, I ask them to leave.

Finally alone, finally not being pelted by rocks or rain or the fascinated stares of strangers, I flop on the bed, face down. I hate Joules's life. I hate the look of it, the smell of it, the feel of this hairy duvet cover up my nose. Nigel's a good guy and all but it makes me so sad to be around him. It's like being around a puppy with three legs. Every time you see that dog you're going to be busted up about how things could have been for him, but here he is, hopping across the carpet toward you with his tongue lolling out of his mouth, not minding the missing leg one bit.

It's too much. I've never felt more alone in my life—if it's even my life any more. I want to go home. I want to be me. I want someone to talk to. I want someone to hold me.

I prop myself up on my elbows and stare at the phone on the nightstand. There's one person I can call who might make me feel normal again. One person who is still himself, whose face I've been staring at for so many years I could close my eyes and draw it. Will Sherwood.

I haven't thought to charge Joules's cellphone all day and now it's dead. Which means I don't have his number.

It's late—nearly eleven-thirty. Far too late to call anyone's house. But I'm so lonely I could die and am willing to face anyone's wrath for a little kindness. I dial 411, jot down the number and pray Will picks up the phone. He doesn't. A woman does. His annoyed-sounding mother.

"I'm sorry to bother you. Is Will there?"

She's a bit nicer now and tells me to hold on a second, says she's not sure he's still up but will go check. A minute or so passes, a few clicks, then Will's voice. "Hey, Joules." He sounds as annoyed as his mother. "If this is to rehash what happened today, I don't have the energy."

I don't know why this does it. He's not my boyfriend, he's barely my friend, but hearing his voice makes me start to sob. Hard. I can barely speak.

"Will?"

"What's wrong?"

"I'm . . . I just . . . ."

"What happened? Did something happen?"

I'm sobbing so hard now I drop my head onto the black pillow. "Can you come here? Do you think you could come here?"

"Are you hurt? Should I call for help?"

"No." I reach for another pillow and wrap my body around it. "I just need someone to hold me."

"I'm on my way."

Half an hour later I am wrapped in him. We haven't

looked at each other, haven't spoken since he climbed through the window and onto Joules's bed. All I've done is cry uncontrollably and all he's done is hold me in silence. I adore him for his quiet presence, for all the things he could be saying, asking right now but isn't. He holds me from behind and strokes my hands, which I have pressed to my chin. Every once in a while he kisses the top of my head. But mostly he's just there.

I want to tell him what has happened. I want to say how stupid I was to want to step into someone else's life, maybe even prove to him I'm Andrea and not his cheating girlfriend. Ex-girlfriend. But you can't tell a person something like that. Even your own mother won't believe you. Will would think it was a crazy prank on Joules's part. He'd think this was a stupid set-up to get him over here so that Joules could have him back again.

Instead, I do the only thing I can do. I be the only person I know how to be—me.

My sobbing has slowed now, and Will rises up on one elbow to look down on me. "Do you want to talk about it?"

I take his free hand in mine and trace the veins on the back. I shake my head.

"But no one hurt you, right? Because then I'd make you tell me."

"No one hurt me." I look at his hand again. There's a scab on his knuckles. "I hope this isn't because of Jou—me."

He almost smiles. "Soccer."

I turn around to face him and lay my arm over his hip. He smells of the shower he must have had earlier this evening. But there's something else. Some sort of fabric softener maybe. In some scent they probably call Ocean Spray or Summer Breeze. It's that thing about families having smells. His mother probably doesn't even realize that, even when they leave the house, her family smells like Ocean Spray. I bet if she did, she'd be glad.

I wonder—if I were to walk into my house tonight, after being gone so long, really gone, would I finally know what it smells like? I move closer to Will and drink in his family.

"What's different about you?" he asks.

I look up. "I don't know."

"It's like something's missing."

Of course. I'm the dulled-down version of her. That star quality Joules normally wears like a skin isn't sustainable with someone like me at the controls.

I've barely said fifty words to Will since the switch and already he can sense it. I don't answer.

"You're . . . softer somehow," he says. "Maybe it's because you've been crying, or because of today, but you're softer."

I manage a sad smile. "Maybe it's this disgusting dead Sasquatch duvet."

He starts to laugh. We both do. Then he looks at me, really looks at me. "Even your eyes. I don't know." He shakes his head and exhales, raising his brows. "It's strange."

"Sorry."

He runs his finger along my shoulder. "Don't apologize."

"But I'm being all weird. I don't want you to think I'm weird."

"I don't. I think you're sweet."

Okay. This is going to take a moment to process. Here I am being myself, not trying to be Joules like before, and Will Sherwood actually likes it? He pushes hair from my face and stares at me. I shift one leg closer so our thighs are touching. He runs his hand down my back.

It's about to happen.

Will Sherwood is about to kiss me.

I've imagined it so many times I could faint from the tension. The smack-in-the-face reality that it is about to happen. Those wide lips, so ready to smile, are about to touch mine. Well, Joules's, but still. Mine for now. Outside the bedroom door, the voices and the music carry on as if nothing has changed. But it has. The entire world has changed. Will Sherwood actually likes me.

Of course, I'm in Joules's shell. What he's liking right now is me in Joules's shell. Which isn't me at all.

He moves closer and lets his eyes close. Just as his lips graze mine, and I lose myself in the sweetest sensation I've ever felt, just as the lightning bolt that is my deepest desire coming true cracks into me and shoots electricity down my spinal cord to my toes, I sit up and gulp for air.

He falls back onto the pillow, confused. "What is it?"

"I don't know." I want to tell him. Look at him lying there, so good and trusting and open. Why shouldn't I tell him the truth? "What do you think about Andrea Birch?"

He groans, covers his eyes with one hand. "Not this again."

I need to know. "Would you ever go out with her?"

"I'm not answering *that!*"

"No, I swear, it's not what you think." I lie down beside him and take his hand again. "This isn't a trap. I'm just curious about how people perceive her. How you perceive her."

"When you asked me yesterday and I told you— you got all upset and started saying crazy stuff about wishing you could switch lives with her, remember? I'm not falling for that again. Why do you keep bring- ing her up, anyway?"

Wait. Joules wished she could switch lives with me?

I sit up and think back to the horrified expression on her face when we spoke about the wish before. "I said that?"

"You don't remember?"

"What time was it?"

"What time? God, I don't know. Last night. You were there."

"No, but where were we?"

"In my basement. It had just started to rain and we came inside. We were watching TV and—"

"What show?"

He sits up and leans back against the wall. "What's this about, Joules?"

"What show was it?"

"I don't know. *The Office,* I think. But we only saw the beginning. Then we started to fight, remember?"

The Office. Monday night. I know it comes on at ten, I watch it with Bray and Cici usually.

Joules made her wish just after ten.

And so did I.

Which means this switch isn't my fault, not fully. Joules is every bit as much to blame as me. This should make me mad—furious!—especially since she's been blaming me all day. But it doesn't. It thrills me to know it wasn't all my doing.

He watches me, shaking his head. "What are you grinning about?"

"I don't know. You're right, I'm crazy tonight."

"I won't argue with that." He starts to pull me closer again. "But I don't mind it. You're not last-night crazy—scary crazy. You're just kind of cute crazy. Sexy crazy."

Did Will Sherwood just call me sexy? And does he mean me or Joules? I need to know. "You mean physically, right?"

"Honestly? Not at all." He tugs on my hair playfully. "I mean you. You're so different. I don't know what's going on but I like it."

I want to kiss him so much my lips hurt. "Enough to undo the breakup?"

"More than enough to undo it."

"We can start fresh? Today is day one?"

"Today is whatever day you want it to be." He pulls on my shoulders. "Now get over here."

I could wrap my arms around his neck. I could nuzzle his earlobe. I could run my hand along his arm. I could have the greatest night of my life. And I could do it without guilt because Joules lied to me about the wish. She cheated on Will, she lied to me, she's mean to her dad—why do I feel I owe this girl so much?

Besides, what's the harm in a little kiss?

I pull away and stand up. "I have to be someplace."

"Now? It's after midnight. Where do you have to go?"

"To Andrea Birch's house."

He exhales hard and falls against the pillows. "I swear to you I wasn't doing anything with her in the music room. I was playing, she came in. End of story. I've been alone with other girls in other classrooms, why are you getting nuts about Andrea? Because of that thing I said?"

Here it is again. I try to sound casual. "What thing was that?"

He stands up and reaches for his car keys. "Now I know you're going insane. Come on, I'll drive you."

"Just tell me—what did you say about Andrea?"

"Ugh." He rolls his eyes. "You really want me to repeat it?"

"Yes."

"Just that there was a time I might have had a bit of a crush."

"A crush on Andrea?"

"Yes, now can we drop it?"

I smile, roll his admission around in my mouth like a caramel and nod once. "Yes."

192

chapter 14

There was no way to get to Joules last night. Will dropped me off at my real house but my bedroom window was locked up tight, and in spite of all my tapping, the girl just lay there in my bed, mouth open, probably drooling on my pillow. Will drove me home without asking any questions about Andrea Birch.

So here I am at school on Thursday for the second day without my body. And want to hear something weird? It's feeling less like someone else's body by the hour. Like a drastic haircut, it's starting to feel normal. What doesn't feel normal is that today kids are looking at me, pointing, whispering. I check my outfit for errors, but with ripped black skinnies, floppy work boots and a white T-shirt I could hardly go wrong. I guess someone might think the studded belt was a bit much if Andrea Birch were wearing it, but as far as the students of Sunnyside High know, she isn't.

More stares from a group of cheerleaders. Two girls in a stairwell giggles.

Is it my hair? I braided it today to keep it off my face during Art class—were braids declared to be a joke overnight? I notice two police cars out on Chapman. No flashing lights or anything exciting, just parked at the side of the road with no one in them. I almost hope they're here to arrest me for the wish.

Joules waits for me by her locker, and from the way she's got her arms crossed and from the look on her Andrea face, it's clear she's plenty mad.

"How did you manage to get the paparazzi interested? I've been trying nearly my whole life."

I open the locker and pull a pencil case down from the shelf. "You're talking to me?"

"Seriously—how?"

"When I tell you my news, you're going to adore me. No kidding. There may even be hugging."

"And what were you and Nige doing in Balboa last night, anyway? The wish probably didn't work because you were off chowing down on pizza at the beach. It probably got stale or something."

"Are you remotely interested in what I have to say? Did I mention it concerns Will?"

The arms are uncrossed, and though she's not quite hugging me, she's tugging on my arm. "What? Tell me!"

I'm feeling a little evil this morning and jump on the chance to torture her. After all, she did lie about her side of the wish. "He's such a nice guy. Have I ever told you how much I admire him?"

"Shut up and tell me. What happened?"

"And he has such an open, friendly face, don't you think?"

She shoves me. "Tell me!"

"I was looking at him last night and I thought, wow, this guy could be in movies. He's just got that likeable boy-next-door quality that female audiences would go for."

"I swear to God, I'll get a dragon tattoo right across your face . . ."

"Okay." I tuck my binder under my arm and turn to face her. "You and Will are back together."

She closes her eyes and leans against the lockers. "Thank you." A deep, relieved sigh parts her lips. *"Thank youthankyouthankyouthankyouthankyouthankyou."* Her eyes fly open; she's horrified now. "Wait. Please tell me you didn't sleep with him!"

"I didn't even kiss him."

"Thank you."

"It wasn't easy, you know. He was really hurt that you cheated."

"I'll never cheat on him again. I swear. Make sure to tell him. Promise?"

A group of niners walk by, again, whispering and staring at me. One of them pulls out a cellphone and takes my picture. I nudge Joules. "What's with everyone? Why are they so fascinated by me today?"

"You don't know?"

I shake my head.

"The paparazzi staked out the restaurant where you and Nige went last night. Your photo was on Perez Hilton this morning." She rolls her eyes. "You and Nige eating pizza, through the window. I've been trying to get on Perez for *ages*. Then you go and get famous your first day as me while I'm waiting in the freaking rain. It's not fair."

That's all? Nigel Adams's daughter is on a gossip website and everyone has to stare? It's not like they haven't been staring at Joules's lousy face for years anyway. This makes her famous?

She continues. "I mean, that photo could travel. It could be in *People* or *In Touch* by Monday. Look at you." She waves her arm toward me and groans. "You're gorgeous."

I watch her, all twisted inside out about missing her shot at fame. "Joules, do you even know why we were there? Do you even know why the paparazzi tailed him?"

"No."

"Because 'Rockabye' went platinum—I told you last night."

"Oh yeah." She stares at the sky and thinks for a moment. "He has plenty of people to celebrate with. He'd have been okay if you'd said you had plans and bailed. I do it all the time and he's totally fine."

"He has people but you're the one he wants to love him. Don't you see that?"

The bell rings and people rush past us to get to class. Joules narrows her eyes and glares at me. "Don't roll around in my world for one day and tell me how to live it, okay? I've been with my dad a lifetime. I think I know him better than you."

Walking backwards, I head toward Art class with her sketchbook pressed to my chest. "Do you, Joules? Really?"

"Of course!"

"What does he take on his pizza, only at Mama Rosa's, that he doesn't usually take?"

She thinks about this a moment, then reddens. "I

don't have time for pizza toppings. I need to get busy analyzing your life like you're analyzing mine."

As she stomps toward the stairs, I call, "The real reason he's getting this press is because he announced all 'Rockabye' proceeds are going to that family with the boy that died. The Glass family. Nigel's a decent guy, Joules. He's worth your time."

"Good to know."

"Everyone sees it but you."

"Later, Dr. Phil."

Later, on my way to Algebra, which is way at the front of campus in no-man's-land, I pass by the little clay-roofed building that houses the office and the library. All around the exterior are these tropical-looking bushes that the custodian always has to water. I see him every morning. With all the rain last night, I wonder if he has to water anyway or if he gets the morning off. Sometimes I watch him and feel bad that he has to empty all the trash cans and everything. Clean up after all of us slobs. It bugs me. I mean, he's an adult; it should be the other way around, but here are all these kids—not super-rich but most of them have it okay—and he has to clean up their balled-up candy bar wrappers and crumpled pop cans. And then there are the teachers who get to sit at desks and write on chalkboards while he's out there with a garbage bag. It makes me think about his mother and what she imagined for him. Probably not this.

It's the kind of thing that depresses me to pieces.

I hear voices outside the office and slow down. As I get closer—close enough to hear what they're saying—I realize Mom is here. The second bell rings but I ignore it, instead heading down the steps to where I can sit on a bench as Joules and pretend to fuss with my shoe.

". . . but they're changes only you can make, Brayden Jacob," Mom says. I look over to see Kaylee and Kaia in the double stroller. Michaela stands behind Mom's legs, still clutching the taffy-colored dog. I notice she's dressed in her sandals and a long T-shirt of Cici's, cinched with a belt. Brayden leans against a railing and stares at his shoes. "Breaking lifelong patterns takes deliberate and determined choices. And I can't make them for you."

Bray mumbles something I can't hear.

"Those friends of yours are good people, but

they're choosing a destructive path. What you have to remember is they are making that choice for themselves. You can choose something else entirely."

Those losers he hangs out with. They must have gotten into trouble again. I've told Mom to make him dump them but you heard her. It's all about choices.

Two policemen come out of the office and I see now that the glass door has been boarded over with plywood. Someone has broken into the office, and from the way the cops are looking at Brayden, it's pretty clear they think he was involved.

Here's the thing about Bray. He's one of these kids who gets too big a kick out of things. He gets bored easily, and if one of his moron friends suggests something illegal, if it's just the slightest bit funny or if Bray has had a dull day, he'll go along with it. He's not a bad kid but he's naive. Always figures, "Ah, we won't get caught." And Mom, she loves him so much and is all about *him* making better choices. But Bray's too immature for that, he's too easily swayed by the promise of a fun night. Maybe one day he'll make smarter choices, but right now he can't. Or won't.

Mom needs to police this kid. He needs to be forbidden to hang with those guys. She sees the decency in everyone, but those guys aren't decent. I try to tell her, but that's Mom. She knows best and, in her eyes, even the most gruesome murderer could change if he'd only remember he is not his past and he has the control to make better choices. Even Charles Manson.

I've tried to talk to Bray. I've pointed out what sort of futures these other guys are setting up for themselves and how he is different. He could have it good. But he winds up calling me Mandrea and I end up pounding him, and then he doesn't take me seriously.

I watch as the principal tells Brayden to head to class. Mom talks to Mr. McCluskey for a bit—the police do too—and then everyone starts to look around as if the conversation is done and they need an excuse to leave. The cops go first, after leaning over and giving the Ks a little poke that makes them giggle and kick their fat, sandaled feet—it's nearly impossible *not* to give the Ks a little poke that makes them giggle and kick their fat, sandaled feet. The principal says goodbye with a half-salute that Mom probably enjoys—he doesn't even look at the twins before he goes, probably because he sees enough kids over the course of a day and can't stand the sight of a couple of possible terrors in the making.

Finally it's just Mom and the girls. But she doesn't

leave right away. In the morning breeze, she pulls a sheet of paper out of the diaper bag, reads it over, then tacks it to the bulletin board beside the office door. Then she reaches into the diaper bag again and gives Kaylee and Kaia each a small plastic container full of Cheerios, which makes their feet even happier than the cops made them.

Mom smiles and it's all I can do to stop myself from running over there, wrapping my Joules arms around her and begging her to believe I am still her daughter. To just accept that sometimes freaky stuff happens and let me come home. I'm not kidding, it hits me so hard in the gut I could throw up.

She slides the sunglasses down from the top of her head onto her nose and, holding Michaela's hand, wheels the babies toward the steps up to the quad, which she will have to cross in order to walk them home. But there are, like, eight steps. She can't possibly get a double stroller up them alone.

I drop my bag and run over to her, grinning like an idiot. I'll help her. I'll lift the front end while she lifts the back and I'll get a few seconds of her to keep me going for the rest of the day. As I approach, I say, "Hi, Mrs. Birch. Can I help you up the stairs?"

She narrows her eyes at me, obviously recognizing me from the other morning in my bedroom with Joules, and takes a step backward as if she's thinking about bolting. Then Mom motions toward the stucco wall, behind which is a ramp I didn't know existed. "Thank you. But I'm okay with the ramp."

Idiotic of me. Of course there's a ramp. How else could a wheelchair or a dolly get down to the office? I can feel my cheeks burn. "Oh, right! I forgot about that."

Mom stares at me through her dark glasses, the wind fluttering her bangs. She's wearing the thin silver necklace I got her for her birthday a few years ago. It's too thin, I know, for an adult to wear, but it was cheap and pretty and I thought it would match her hair. Anyway, she wears it all the time. If she ever thought it was stupidly thin, she never mentioned it.

"Your babies are adorable," I say, leaning over to squeeze Kaia's sandal. "You're a little cutie, aren't you?"

Kaia laughs, kicks at me playfully and says, "Again! Again!"

Kaylee sets her Cheerios on her lap and holds up her chubby arms. "Up!"

How I would love to pick her up.

Mom laughs and pulls the stroller away, with some

struggle, and points it toward the ramp. "Thanks for your offer. You have a nice afternoon now." Without another word, she wheels the girls away.

Out on the street, a car honks. Traffic roars past. I stand there, staring at them until the principal comes out of the office again, walks past me and mutters, "Second bell has rung, Miss Adams. Get into the office and get yourself a late slip."

I wander back to where I dropped Joules's bag.

Before I head into the office, I stop at the bulletin board to see what Mom posted. It's one of those flyers where the bottom is cut into phone number tabs you can pull off and take with you. What it says thumps me in the stomach: "Mother's Helper Wanted."

Which means two very rotten things. Joules is being no help with the kids. And Andrea Birch is being replaced.

I rip off a tab and slip it into my pocket.

chapter 15

Our house on Highcliffe Court doesn't sit square on the lot. I mean, this entire neighborhood was built on a hillside with one main road winding to the top, and shooting off to both sides are stubby cul-de-sacs where each house is placed according to the slope. Our house is on a pie-shaped lot with the hill rising straight up in the back, so the house is turned away from the street a bit. Which sometimes makes people confused. Often they come to our side door thinking it's the front. It drives Mom nuts because the den is right there, so she might be inside folding laundry and all of a sudden the door beside her starts banging.

Today it works well for me. Fully aware that Mom is a bit suspicious of Joules, I decide that getting Dad onside first might increase my chances of getting hired as the Mother's Helper. Besides that, I miss him. I want to see him.

It's just after six o'clock, Thursday night. With any luck, Dad will be taking command of the weather in the den while Mom is in the front of the house fussing with dinner.

I knock on the side door and almost instantly it flies open. Dad stands there, all red-headed and buzz cut, his droopy face all friendly and his feet all slippered. Behind him I can hear the music from The Weather Show. It's the song they play every ten minutes when they show the local weather in stages of what's happening right now, what'll be happening the rest of the day, then the next three days, the next week and the next two weeks. Usually all you see is a little illustration of the sun. Sometimes Dad gets lucky and there's a teensy drawing of a cloud beside the sun. But that's mostly it.

He rubs the top of his head with his palm and smiles. "Well there. What can I do ya for?"

I can't resist. It'll make him so happy. "Umm, I was wondering if you have the time. The exact time."

You can't believe how high his eyebrows shoot up. The man is thrilled. He pushes up his sleeve and consults his watch, pushing a few buttons. "I surely do." After a squint, he announces, "It is six-oh-eight, my dear. Universal Time."

"Oh, thanks. I'm actually here about the Mother's Helper position. Is it filled yet?"

This makes him even happier. He opens the door wide and motions for me to come in. "It most certainly is not. The boss isn't home just yet but you can leave a bit of information for her. She'll be thrilled that you stopped by."

I follow him into the den and take a deep breath, trying to drink my life in. If I was hoping to detect a smell, I'm disappointed. It hasn't been long enough. My life still smells like nothing.

He pulls out a chair at the folding card table set up by the far wall and he lowers the volume of The Weather Show without turning it off. "I'm Gary Birch. And you are?"

"Joules Adams."

"Good, good." He sneaks a peek at the TV and frowns, then looks back at me. "So you're looking for a part-time job, are you, Joules?"

"Yes. Working with children."

He laughs. "Well, you came to the right place for that. You have any experience babysitting? Do you have your certificate?"

I nod. "Both, yes. I've watched kids of all ages."

"You live nearby?"

"Just over on Skyline."

He whistles like he's impressed. "Some gorgeous properties up on that hillside. You have a good view from your place?"

"Pretty nice. But I think I like your house better."

This thrills him right down to the sheepskin slippers. "Well, now, isn't that interesting. You see straight through to the next town from your place?"

I shrug. I can see him processing this: the possibilities of seeing straight across to another county to keep track of not only his own pressure system but his neighbors'.

"Well, I think the big boss is going to like you just fine, Joules. I might even put in a good word for you." He winks. "We have a daughter about your age. Andrea. You see her around school?"

"Um . . ."

The sound of grocery bags comes from the kitchen. About a second later, Mom's head pops around the corner. "Who are you talking—?" Her face falls when she sees me. "Oh. Hello."

"Honey, we have here our very first applicant for the position of Mother's Helper. All chock-full of experience and training and what have you. I'm sold on Joules. What do you say? Should we give her a try?"

Silently, I beg. Silently, I plead. It's the only way I know—until I figure things out—to get back into this house, at least part-time. I can help with Bray—whose crush on Joules Adams might finally come in handy. He might actually listen to what she has to say about his friends. I can listen to my dad's slippers padding around the back room. I can see the way the Ks settle right down after their bath because they know Mom is going to sing them "Rock-a-bye, Baby."

I can try to figure out if they really do know who I am. Mom has to say yes. She has to.

I throw him a big smile. "I actually love working with kids. I can sterilize bottles, change diapers, wash sheets, watch them at the playground. Anything at all. Help with dinner."

Dad winks at Mom like hiring me is in the bag. "Tell me, Miss Joules, what do you charge?"

"Anything. I don't even care. You don't even have to pay me at all. I just love kids."

He laughs. "Oh, don't you worry. If you do the work, you reap the rewards. I think we agreed on seven dollars an hour, didn't we, hon?"

Mom smiles politely. "Well, let's not get ahead of ourselves. I'm not sure it's such a good idea to hire a friend of Andrea's."

Dad leans back and looks at me as if I've turned into a monkey. "You're friends with our Andrea?"

"Well, yes, I—"

Mom says, "Joules was here yesterday morning, when she and Andrea went to the bridge." She looks at me, analyzes me.

I smile. "I know it looked weird. It was this stupid kid thing. We wanted to make a wish come true. Idiotic. It was my idea, not hers. A bad choice. And I'm sorry if I trampled your flowers."

Mom seems almost willing to forgive and see me in a different light. Not quite, but almost.

"We all have to make choices," I add, hoping to hit her in her soft spot. "And I'm trying to make some good ones for once. Trying to make sure I don't repeat the poor choices of my past. It's what life is about, right?"

It's worked. I can tell by the way Mom has tilted her body toward me. She leans against the door frame. "And you say you have training?"

I nod yes at the same time Joules's cellphone rings loudly from her purse. I ignore it. "I do. And the instructor said I was the best . . ."

Dad points toward the phone, which is still ringing. "Go ahead and get that."

"No, it's okay. My instructor said I—"

Mom said, "You'd better get your phone. It could be important. It could be your parents."

With Joules's phone, it could be anyone—Shane, even. I really don't want to answer it right here, right now, when I'm on the verge of getting hired back into my life. Then again, if I don't, Mom will take it that I don't care about my parents and she'll think I'm not family oriented. I have no choice. Praying the call is a wrong number, I flip open the phone. "Hello?"

The connection is so loud I have to hold the phone away from my ear. Nigel's voice says, "That you, missie?" When I say loud, I mean loud. Mom and Dad can hear him for sure. I wish Dad would up the volume on the TV or someone would have a coughing fit or something. Anything to drown out Nigel.

"Jujube—you there?"

"Yes, Nigel. I'm here."

"Now what did we say about calling me names that make me sound like a shallow rock star?"

Mom and Dad look at each other and smile.

"Dad, I'm kind of busy right now." Why does Joules have the stupid volume set so high? I scramble to find a way to turn it down.

"Listen, pumpkin," Nigel's voice booms through

the back room. It's as if he's here with us, shouting as loud as he can. Mom and Dad start fussing with things on the table to make like they're not listening, but they hear him. Boy, do they hear him. Dad even starts to joke around and cover his ears.

"Bit of a glitch," Nigel shouts. "It's all a matter of red tape and legal garbage, ridiculous really. You'd think these wankers would spend their time arresting actual criminals, but baby, I need to let you know what's going on. I'm in jail."

chapter 16

I didn't get the job.

Mom didn't come right out and say it but it was pretty clear from the way her mouth crushed itself into the shape of a flattened bicycle tire. If there is anyone, anywhere, Mom doesn't approve of it's a parent who "abuses their God-given privilege to care for a child." And I'm guessing Mom thinks it's pretty hard to care for a child from the inside of a prison cell.

One year this teeny tiny newborn baby girl came to us. Lee-Ann, her mother called her, if you could call this woman a mother. I don't often see them, the parents of the foster kids. It's usually the lady in the flowered pants who drops off and picks up. But after Lee-Ann came—a long time later, three months or maybe four—I started to see this beat-up old car sitting outside the house. In it was a nervous lady, kind of young, really skinny with scraggly yellow hair and the kind of teeth that push out your lower lip. She wore all this blue glop on her slitty eyes and smoked nonstop.

I'd see her on my way home from school, not every day or anything but often enough. She never made like she was watching our house. When I walked past she got busy lighting another cigarette or examining her nails or digging through her glove compartment. But come on, there are only four houses on our cul-de-sac and only one of them houses the abused offspring of lousy parents. It didn't take a genius to figure out who she was, what she was up to. She wanted to catch a glimpse of her baby. When I got real close she'd always look up as if she was surprised to see someone and flash me a smile with these scary chipped teeth.

Lee-Ann was a really well-behaved baby as far as babies go. Slept through the night, never fussed, loved bath time. The weird thing about her was that she never cried. I didn't even think that was possible for a baby—to never cry, not even once. Even when Mom and I took her to the doctor for shots, the doctor poked her with the needle and nothing. Lee-Ann just looked at him and blinked.

I thought she was some kind of super-baby, but

one time late at night I got up to get a drink of water from the kitchen and overheard Mom and Dad talking in the back room. They were talking about Lee-Ann's mother and why Lee-Ann never cried. The woman in the car, apparently, used to go out and leave Lee-Ann all alone. Sometimes for hours. So here was this baby who at first probably cried and cried in the hope that her mother would respond, but eventually she just gave up. She learned crying doesn't get you much in life and stopped bothering. The night the flowered pants lady took her into foster care, the mother had left the house in the evening and not come home until six the next morning. By that time her neighbors had figured out what was happening. The police had broken into the place, given Lee-Ann to the Child Services people and were waiting for the mother at the kitchen table.

You should have heard Mom go on about that mother. Called her a nasty piece of business who should get sterilized already. Mom said that if she ran the show she'd ensure certain people, once they'd proven themselves to be abusive or neglectful to a child, be sterilized by law.

Her forgiving attitude toward wayward fosters does not extend to lousy parents.

But here's the strange thing. It made me feel so sad for the lady with the chipped teeth. I couldn't stop thinking about the way she'd go hunting through the glove box, then look up and flash me that broken smile. Don't get me wrong, I get why Mom was upset. But there was something so childlike about that smile. As if she wasn't much older than Lee-Ann herself or something.

Anyway. There's no way Mom will bring me into the house to care for the children now. I've been tainted by Nigel's arrest.

I walk back to Skyline Drive more slowly than I've ever walked in my life. There's no reason to hurry. I'm not all that excited to find out what, exactly, Nigel did to land himself in jail—and why did he have to go and do something stupid anyway? Here's the world thinking he has it so good: big rock star guy, totally generous, his song just goes platinum. But the truth is he doesn't. How could he—he lives with a daughter who couldn't care less about any of it.

The house is dark when I arrive. No surprise, I guess. Nigel is, as they say, detained. I dig through Joules's purse for keys and come up empty. Great. Just freaking great. I walk around the house, stepping over the bushes, and catch the first bit of luck

I've had in days. The bedroom window isn't locked.
I climb inside, fall into Joules's bed and go to sleep.

When I wake Friday morning the house is full of
people. I can hear loud voices coming from the
kitchen, along with the sounds of cupboard doors
slamming and pots and pans clashing. Nigel must be
home.

I forgot to close the bedroom window last night
and the wind blowing in is cool. I shower, floss
Joules's precious teeth like she begged me to and pull
on a thick cotton sweater and jeans. Maybe I feel like
I'm going into battle or something, because I reach
for a pair of tough-looking motorcycle boots and slip
my feet into them. With my hair still damp, I head
into the kitchen.

I don't know what I was expecting, maybe another
party, but the atmosphere in the kitchen is serious.
Newspapers are spread out across the island where
Nigel sits looking terrible in a sweatshirt and jeans.
Bare feet with hairy toes. When he sees me, he half
smiles. "Hey there, kitten. I hope we didn't wake
you."

About six or seven men and women drip from counters and stools, or lean against the table. Some are on cellphones, one guy is rooting through the fridge, two women are madly writing on pads of paper.

"What's going on?" I say.

"You know Eddie. Clara, Sue, Aidan and the Hendridge boys. Old Nige's Dream Team." He motioned toward each as he said their names. "We're building me a new image."

"How did you get out so fast?" I ask.

"Bailed myself out."

The short, muscled guy Nigel introduced as Eddie, in a tight black T and gelled hair, picks up one of the papers and raises his eyebrows at Nigel. When Nige nods, Eddie tosses it onto the island close to me. There, on the front page, is a huge picture of Nigel. A mug shot in which his eyes are only half open, his cheeks are sunken in, and his hair is a mess. The headline reads "Nigel Adams Arrested for DUI."

Driving under the influence. Drinking and driving—of course. He did it the other night, when I was with him.

"We're doing a bit of damage control here," Eddie says. He nods toward the two women with the notepads. "Nothing Nige's brilliant publicists can't handle."

A tray of coffees appears atop the newspapers and everyone reaches for one. There seems to be one for me left over so I take it and sip. Sure enough, it's spiked. I set it down again, once again disappointed that Nigel is willing to go to such lengths to make his daughter love him.

"I'm screwed," Nigel says into his coffee cup. "Mel Gibson screwed. Look at that photo. It'll be seared into people's minds forever."

An older guy with long hair and ripped jeans laughs. "You ain't pretty, dude."

"Hey," says Nige. "It was the middle of the night."

"It was barely six o'clock. In the evening."

"What happened, exactly?" I ask. "Were you drinking champagne again to celebrate or what?"

Nigel waves my question away. "I wasn't doing anything that would hurt anybody. I'd had a few sips over a late lunch and got pulled over on the freeway. Not because I was too wasted to drive. I was fine. I'd just dropped my CD and was fishing around for it on the floor. Damned cops just needed a celebrity to make an example of, that's all."

Eddie and the other guys start shaking their heads in anger, completely offended on Nigel's behalf.

"How many drinks had you had?" I ask. "Did the police have you blow into the breathalyzer?"

"Those things are never accurate," Eddie says. "The cops set them high so they can meet their arrest quota for the month. It's all a big money-grab."

A tall blonde with a headpiece in her ear—Sue, I believe, one of the publicists—brings her notes over from the table. She's very competent-looking, dressed sharp with her hair pulled back in an efficient ponytail. "Clara and I have got it all worked out," she says after sipping her coffee. "America loves a comeback." She looks at Nigel, hunched over a piece of toast, his hair pointed every which way, his face more wrinkled than ever. "Celebrity makes a bad choice. Celebrity repents, shows himself to be serious by checking himself into rehab and comes out humble and full of remorse but determined to keep himself on the straight and narrow in the future. It happens all the time."

Nigel thinks about this. "Rehab?" He laughs. "No way. Seriously, I messed up but I don't need rehab."

"I agree," Sue says. "You won't go to rehab. But the world will think you've gone to rehab. There are many, many facilities in many, many countries. All we need is a good photo of you hugging your daughter goodbye as you get on a plane. Believe me, we'll make it look so real the pilot himself will be weeping."

"Wait," I say. "I have to get on a plane? I've never been on a plane!"

Nigel looks at me like I'm high, then starts laughing. "You're killing me, Jujube. Seriously." He sips from his probably rum-soaked coffee and wipes his mouth. "Never been on a plane!"

"You won't be flying anywhere," Sue explains to me. "Nigel boards the plane while paparazzi snap pictures they will then sell to *People* magazine, *In Touch* and *Star.* You'll wave at him from the tarmac and look every bit the loving daughter of the most generous man on earth. The plane will be sealed up, it will taxi away from the gate, and the paparazzi will leave and go sell their photos for megabucks."

"But where will the plane go?"

The other publicist—the shorter one with the dark bob, Clara—stands up and stretches. "The plane will pull into a hangar on the other side of the airport. Nigel will exit in disguise and step straight into a limo. A few hours later, once it's nice and dark out, a different car will pull into your garage and your dad will hole up in the house for the next twenty-eight days."

Sue says, "Nigel reemerges a changed man. He appears looking healthy on a few magazine covers and we sell the exclusive story to *People* magazine for hundreds of thousands of dollars, positioning him as the wholesome, loving father who is asking his daughter's forgiveness. America will eat it up. It's a no-fail scenario. Nigel will become the most read-about musician of the year."

Nigel starts to nod, clearly in favor of the scheme. "It's like I always say, for every itch there's a scratch. And this, my friends, is one hell of a brilliant scratch."

Eddie rubs his hands together. "Ca-ching. I like the sound of all this publicity. It'll sell a lot of records."

"You oughta be my agent, Eddie," says Nigel.

"I am your agent, dude."

"So?" says Clara. "What do you think, Nigel?"

Nigel frowns a minute. "Most read-about musician of the year, you say?"

"That's right."

He sits back in his seat and clasps his hands behind his head. Then he nods. "I like it."

Everyone is grinning like it's the most genius plan on earth. Then Eddie starts to clap very slowly. One by one, they all join in until the whole freaking room is clapping for Sue and Clara, who laugh and take these fake bows in front of Nigel.

When things quiet down, Sue puts her arm around

my shoulders. "The key to pulling this off is this beautiful young girl here. What do you say, Joules? Want to help your darling father out of the terrible mess the police have put him in?"

No, I want to say. *I don't. I don't want any part of this ugly lie.* And no one put him in any mess, he did it to himself. He drank too much, drove, got caught and now has to suffer the consequences just like any other criminal.

Nigel watches me with this big worried smile on his face.

Any other father—a father like my own—would stand up and say no way. My daughter is not going to lie to cover up my own mistakes. Nigel doesn't. But that isn't what's bugging me right now. Nor is it that Nigel messed up in the first place—that bugs me, but not as much as this.

The smile on Nigel's face isn't the smile of a spoiled-rotten rock star who is used to getting his way. It's the smile of a father who *really* wants to believe his daughter loves him. Other dads—dads who are waiters and engineers and daycare workers and bottled water delivery guys—might go about their business with the security of knowing their kids love them wholly. But not Nigel. Not the guy whose publicist says he'll be the most read-about musician and father on the planet.

His daughter can't disappoint him, no matter how immoral their plan. Joules can't let him down in front of all these people. It would devastate him.

I walk around to where he sits, put my arms around his shoulders and kiss him on the cheek. "Of course I'll help. I would do anything for this old guy."

He beams. Looks at me, looks at his people, and just beams and beams and beams. Then he laughs, reaches for a tea towel and pretends to snap me with it for calling him an old guy. He chases me around the kitchen, roaring. At this moment, he just might be the happiest father in America.

•

I don't go to school at all today. One of the publicists calls in and says I have a family emergency. So instead of fighting with Joules, staring at Will and hoping to catch a glimpse of my mother in the parking lot, I pose for father–daughter pictures with Nigel. Me and him packing his bag. Me and him at the piano as he sings me a goodbye song. Then, later, at the airport, there will be me and Nigel hugging beside a private plane. This photo will not be shot by Clara and Sue, however. One of them called the paparazzi and claimed to be Nigel's snitch of a housekeeper who wanted to give them a tip: that Nigel would be at LAX, at Gate 13C, 4:45 p.m. sharp. Sure enough, the photographers are there when we pull up.

Nigel and I stand on the tarmac, drinking in jet fumes. It's cool again now that the sun is getting low in the sky, and I'm under-dressed. I didn't realize how windy it can get out at the airport—mostly because I've never been to the airport. A fake flight attendant keeps poking her head out of the plane, which has its engines roaring. At first we just sort of stand there on the steps up to the jet, looking like morons, but then Sue—who's about a hundred yards away in a car—flashes the headlights to signal to us that enough paparazzi have shown up. Then Nigel moves into action.

He pretends to tell the flight attendant that the plane has to wait because he has to say goodbye to his daughter. He sets his hands on my shoulders and looks into my eyes as fuel-infused wind blows all around us. To be honest, even if he was saying goodbye, I wouldn't be able to hear him over the sound of the jet engines. Nigel blinks hard as if he's crying and pulls me close. Then he steps back to take one last look at me. He acts all remorseful, as if he's thinking he just doesn't deserve a daughter like me.

I swear to God, Nigel Adams could be an actor. He could win an Academy Award for this performance.

He starts talking to me—no doubt the paparazzi are supposed to think he's apologizing, explaining how long he'll be gone and how it'll be different once he's back. Telling me he'll miss me. But really he's saying this: "Have you heard about that new Chinese place over on Chapman? The egg rolls are supposed to be incredible." Then he looks out at the horizon and shakes his head, so sad. "Let's have Eddie pick some up on the way home, what do you say?"

I wrap my arms around him and bury my face in his sweatshirt. "Sounds good. Can we get egg drop soup? And cashew chicken?"

He backs away, gives me a wave. "For sure. I've invited Clara and Sue back to the house. We'll make a party out of it." After blowing me a kiss, he disappears into the plane and the flight attendant bangs the door shut.

The walk down the rickety metal steps is rough with all those photographers pointing their cameras at me. I keep my head down as if I'm sad—which is fairly easy since I'm terrified—and make my way to where Clara and Sue wait in the town car with its tinted windows. Then I turn to watch the plane begin to move and I wave and wave and wave until the jet has pulled out of sight.

When I climb into the backseat, Clara and Sue turn around and smile. "You did great. Just great," says Clara.

"Absolutely. A flawless performance." Sue stuffs a couple of tortilla chips into her mouth and passes me the bag. "I'm starved, what about you guys? Shall we order a round of pizzas to meet us back at the house?"

"Chinese," I say, taking a handful of chips.

"What's that?" Sue asks as she pulls the car down a lane that will lead us out of LAX. A plane is taking off and the roar has rushed through the open windows. "What'd you say?"

"I said Nigel wants Chinese," I shout.

"Decision made, then," says Clara. "What Nigel needs, Nigel gets."

I stare out the window at the passing cars, pedestrians, baggage carts full of luggage, palm trees, fuchsia flowers, white buildings. It isn't true, what Clara said about Nigel. I wish it was true, but it isn't.

chapter 17

Monday morning my face is everywhere. On the front page of the *L.A. Times,* on covers of gossip magazines, even *People,* it's the same photo: a zoom-in close-up of Joules's face as Nigel hugs me on the roll-away steps beside the plane. I must have looked devastated as Nigel was talking about egg rolls because that's the shot every paper and magazine chose, and it doesn't even show his face.

If I thought life was weird as Joules before, it's completely insane now.

The house is surrounded by photographers, some of whom I recognize from the airport. And since Nigel is supposed to be in rehab we've had to keep the curtains shut tight all weekend. Clara and Sue have been bringing in food, as well as booze disguised in cartons meant for paper towels and macaroni. The neighbors are unimpressed and have called the cops about a zillion times because they can't get in and out of their driveways, and because they keep finding photographers peeing in their azaleas or off the side of the canyon across the street.

I tried to leave the house twice on Sunday, but both times someone shouted, "It's her!" and cameras started clicking like mad. One photographer hopped on his motorcycle and got ready to chase me, most likely in hopes I would lead him to Nigel's secret hideaway. Little did anyone know the great one was about fifteen feet away, in the den watching baseball, flicking beer caps and eating Cheetos. Both times, I ducked back inside and slammed the door. Where could I possibly go with these guys following me?

So today, there is even more excitement, I guess because they figure Joules has to leave the house to go to school. Sue, who might actually be getting used to the attention, and who is probably hoping someone will snap *her* picture and slap it on a magazine cover, volunteers to drive me. It's scary, sitting in the backseat as she navigates through the crowd in the driveway—in reverse. These guys don't clear out of the way. They lean right over the trunk of the car and start taking pictures of me with no concern whatsoever about the car rolling over their feet.

As we cruise along State College, a great thing happens. There's another roadblock that takes traffic down to one lane. The police are looking at every car as it passes between two cop cars, and the paparazzi behind us are forced to let other cars in ahead of them.

"Is this for the black SUV?" I ask.

"It's happening all across Orange County. They're calling it a registration check but yes. You know, they're looking for the person who hit that couple over by Disneyland."

We cruise past the police, who are uninterested in our sedan but give a throwaway glance at our front license plate for good measure.

"I guess they haven't caught the person yet?"

"Nope. I'm sure the driver is long gone anyway. Too much media attention in this state."

"I guess so."

"Sad about those parents," she says, switching lanes. "I heard on the radio this morning they're still in the hospital."

It feels like a boulder has dropped into my stomach. I picture Michaela, wrapped around Mom's neck the first night. "Are they going to live?"

Sue shrugs. "Report just said they're in ICU."

Then she guns the engine and the car shoots forward. "Say goodbye to our photographer friends, Joules."

I look back to see the first of them, sure enough in a dark SUV, being forced to roll down his window and answer a few questions. Which gives us plenty of time to lose them.

It's weird . . . when you look at celebrities, you think it must be so amazing to live their lifestyles. But honestly, if this is what it's like, count me out. It's scary to have these people chasing after you. Their cars and motorcycles follow so close you'd swear you're about to be rear-ended. Plus, forget about scratching your nose or adjusting your underwear. You're on display.

I'm glad they're gone.

Sadly, I guess it wasn't too hard for them to figure out where Joules goes to school since there's just the one high school for the district. More photographers are waiting on Orange Road outside the school. As Sue pulls into the parking lot she says, "Remember, your dad isn't at home. He's in a very exclusive facility that you are not at liberty to reveal."

"Got it."

"If anyone asks if he's in the country, say no. And feel free to play with the paparazzi. Be coy. Tell them Nige may or may not be in Europe, or northern Canada, something like that. Or say this rehab facility is so exclusive they only take a few patients at a time."

The principal and Mr. Mansouri are in the parking lot now, shooing away the photographers. I start to open the door. "I don't think I'll actually talk to them, if that's okay."

Sue spins around to look at me, clearly surprised. "Really? Okay, whatever you want. But enjoy all the attention, sweetie. You're on top of the world today. You're the girl the rest of us want to be."

I climb out and try to ignore the photographers, who are moving closer and chattering excitedly. Some of them call out questions: "Where's your dad, Joules?" and "When's Nigel coming home, darlin'?"

I lean into Sue's window and look at her and say sadly, "I'm not."

"What?"

"I'm not the girl I want to be."

Then—what choice do I have?—with Mr. Mansouri and the principal yelling at the photographers and threatening to call the police if they don't step off school property, I hurry past the crowd and duck my head as they shout out questions: "Where's your father?" "Do you miss Nigel?" "Do you think he can get sober?"

If I thought the situation was scary before, from within the safety of a locked vehicle, it's about fifty times more terrifying on foot. My shoulders actually rub against one guy he gets so close—what is he trying to do, get a shot right up my nose? And I can't escape them. Even if they get kicked off school property, I can see them with their telephoto lenses from across the street.

As I rush toward Leighton Auditorium, I notice Will waving me toward him.

"Follow me." He grabs my hand and we run along an outdoor hallway that stretches the length of the auditorium. He leads me down some steps and motions toward a huge grouping of piney bushes with twisted, crippled trunks and plenty of bare space beneath for us to climb inside. We both fall to the bare earth and peek out beneath the greenery to see what's going on over on Chapman.

He grins, leaning on his elbows. "So, what, you're telling me this new and improved Joules Adams lies down in dirt now?" He pokes me in the side. "What happened to that girlish aversion to things that go bump in the mud? You used to be petrified of insects."

I shrug. What's a little pill bug when you've changed hundreds—and I do mean hundreds—

of diapers? Please. At least bugs aren't covered in human excrement. "What can I say, William Benjamin Hugo Sherwood? I'm an enigma."

His brows shoot skyward. "An enigma who knows my terrible second middle name?"

I laugh a little and roll onto my side to face him. "Seriously. What were your parents thinking?"

"I've never told you that. I've never told *anyone* that. How did you find out?"

When I was over at his house that day working on our school project, it was kind of cold and we were making hot chocolate—those little packets that you mix with boiling water. I had finished my work so I volunteered to heat the water and do the mixing. While I waited, I looked around the room and tried to commit to memory every detail of the place he grew up in. There was a little stack of mail on the counter that had spilled over, and right there on the top was a letter from the school to William Benjamin Hugo Sherwood. A girl obsessed doesn't forget a detail like that, not even three years later.

"I have my ways."

"Sneak."

"Hugo."

He laughs, but his cheeks are tomato red and it makes me feel bad for teasing him.

"Come on, I'm serious," he says, growing more anxious. "I don't want that to get around."

The expression on his face is starting to resemble fear now. It makes me realize something. Even with things going well between us—or between Will and Joules—he is still afraid to fully trust her. He isn't quite sure what his girlfriend will do with this information. I lean closer to poke him playfully in the arm. "I swear, I won't tell anyone."

And the fear melts away from his features. He shoots me this super-appreciative half-grin that says he really does see me—Joules—as someone he could care about. It sends a gush of warmth from my chest to my toes. "Thanks, Joules," he says.

I smile and look down. The pressure of this moment is mammoth. Here we are, hidden away, our faces not even twelve inches apart, and the kiss I've imagined sits all around us like a glass bubble. One false move and I shatter it. The urge to babble idiotic nonsense is rising up my esophagus and onto my tongue but I clamp my lips shut so I don't start yammering on about the lumpiness of the root beneath my stomach and how we'll need to get late slips and what sort of excuse we can use for why we're late because we can't exactly say we were lying in the bushes. Believe me, if I open my mouth right now, that's what will come out.

So I say nothing at all.

The silence I hope will inspire the kiss starts to fester and stink instead. Will blows hair out of his eyes and changes the subject. "So, yeah. You sure know how to stir up a Monday morning with all those photographers."

I nod, disappointed. "I had to shower with the bathroom curtains shut in case these guys were crawling down the hillside with telephoto lenses."

"Good thing you're semi used to it. Anybody else would be a wreck."

I am anybody else, I want to say. *I am a wreck.*

"Who do you have staying with you at the house while Nigel is away?" he asks. "You're not alone, I hope."

I roll my eyes, grinning. "Who do you think?"

"Seriously? All of this is fake?"

"Yup. He watched baseball all day yesterday, drank beer, ate leftover Chinese."

"Are you kidding?"

"Nope."

"He's been at home all this time? So, the getting on the plane thing, the sad expressions, the waving goodbye—that was all pretend?"

"A hundred percent."

He shakes his head in disbelief. "Wow. He put on quite a show. You did too."

"Yeah, well, I'm not proud of it, believe me."

We stare at each other in silence for a moment. Then he looks away and blushes. "I can't believe you know about Hugo. I can never look you in the face again."

I shimmy a bit closer and let my chin drop onto his shoulder. "Don't look away, WBHC. I think it's cute."

This mischievous smile spreads across his face and he rolls me onto my back and tackles me, trapping me with a knee across my lower half. The weight of his leg, the umbrella of leaves, the feel of his breath on my cheek, it's so intense I could burst. My skin is hot and tingles shoot through my body.

He pushes my hair off my cheek and I could faint from his touch. *Kiss me,* I want to scream. *Kiss me!*

Suddenly, I don't care what I've promised Joules. Will and I are hidden. No one will ever know it happened. Joules will never find out. It's the chance of a lifetime, to kiss the one boy I've crushed on for years. I'm Joules, it's not even cheating. Besides, wouldn't it all be in the interests of securing him for her?

He trails one finger along my hip and shakes his

head as if he too is floored by what's happening. "Joules . . ."

I let my lips brush against his jawline. "I know."

He closes his eyes and groans softly.

There's no going back now. I wouldn't stop what is about to happen even if it meant being Joules forever. It would be an even trade. I push my body against his and feel his hand move under my shirt and slide up my back.

Then it happens.

There's a grunt or a gasp outside of the bushes, I'm aware someone is there, and suddenly the weight and warmth of Will's thigh is gone and my legs are cold. We're being pushed apart. I look up just in time to see Joules dive down between us and get her shoulder in my ribs as she drops.

Will stares, shocked, as Andrea Birch props herself up on her elbows and shoots each of us an angry grin. "Aren't you guys way late for class?"

"Hey, we're, uh, we were kind of in the middle of something here," says Will, eyeing me as if to ask if I invited her.

"Yeah? Cool, I'm bored. That's what it's like to be Andie Birch," she says. "B-O-R-I-N-G."

I see what she's doing here. She's trying to make

me look like an idiot for when we switch back. I snort. "Then maybe *you* should get to class. Isn't Mrs. Leonard passing back the tests today?"

"I'm thinking it'll be more fun if you walk me there. *Joules.*"

She wants to separate me from Will, I get that. But she destroyed what was quite possibly the greatest moment of my life, and part of me wants her to pay. "Nah. I'm good."

"She'll see you in class, Andrea," Will says. "We just need a minute."

Her head snaps around to face me. The look in her eyes is pure wickedness. "Walk me there, now. *Joules.*"

"Walk there yourself. *Andrea.*"

Will watches me, confused.

Joules rolls onto her back between us and lets one of her hands caress her belly. "Guys, how do you know if you're pregnant? And is it bad for the baby if you do it a few more times once you've conceived?"

"You are NOT pregnant, Andrea. You're not that kind of girl."

"I don't know. These days I think I kind of am. I've been in the bushes with Shane so many times, you know? And little Stewie Mercer. And Alan King.

tish cohen

And what's-his-name from the cafeteria—you know, the one who can't work the cash machine so they make him stack boxes in the back? The one who pulls his hairnet right down over his eyebrows?"

I grab her arm, haul her out of the bushes and, after an apologetic glance back at Will, I march her toward English. "I was just getting him back for you, you idiot. Nothing happened yet."

"Looked like lots was happening. A deal's a deal, Birch Tree."

"I've been going through hell all weekend. Excuse me if I actually enjoy getting your boyfriend back. You have no idea how much good I'm doing for your life."

"You think I enjoy yours? That Brayden kid keeps going on about how smokin' Joules Adams is—did you know he had the hots for me?"

"Of course!"

She shudders. "And those short people with the diapers! Why do I have to do all the changing from the time I get home? Sam completely reeks of some kind of candy floss lip gloss. And the stuff in your closet—seriously. You have almost nothing to wear. I swear to God, if I have to live one more day in your life I'm offing myself."

"And now when we switch back, Will's going to think I'm a slut!"

She smiles coyly. "He won't. I'll keep him so busy he'll never think of you again. There. Problem solved."

"What about Bray? Did Mom ground him for the office break-in?"

"Are you kidding? Your dad gave him some yard work but your mother thinks he just needs counseling. She keeps saying things like, 'You are better than your past, Brayden. You can only rise above it if you choose to.' Crap like that. He totally takes advantage."

"It's his friends. I don't trust them, you know?"

She nods. "Tomas and Dillon? They're not so bad. Neither is the little one—Ace, is it?"

"I've seen the way they look at our things when they're over. And Mom's bracelet went missing a few months ago. I swear that Tomas kid took it."

Joules starts laughing. "You're such a dreamer, Birchie. Like anyone in their right mind would want to grab anything from your house. The whole place is covered in crushed Cheerios and vomit and work charts, and all your freaking TV plays is The Weather Show. Believe me, your belongings are safe."

It's too much. I can't take hearing about any of it.

I want my life back. My eyes tear up and now I feel sick about being willing to swap my entire family for a moment with a boy.

Joules looks at me and hisses, "Stop it. Joules Adams does not blubber at school."

I step behind a huge arched column and lean over the rail so no one can see me. "I'm tired of this. I want to switch back."

"People will see you. *Me*. Cut it out!"

"I can't stand it any more. And what if we never figure out how to undo it?"

"We will. We totally will."

"You don't know that."

"I do know you have to think positive. Believe it."

"Yeah, I tried that the last time and look where that got us."

She thinks about it a minute, then brightens. "I know. What if we do the *Wizard of Oz* thing. Tap our heels together and say 'No place like home,' like Dorothy and Toto."

"This isn't a movie, Joules. It's real life."

"It's worth a try. You don't seem to have any better ideas."

"Don't be an idiot! That story is pure fiction. And Dorothy had the witch's ruby slippers."

She laughs sadly. "Yeah. We need some glittery red shoes."

Glitter. Wait a minute.

Gran's gloves—I'd forgotten all about them. I was wearing them when I made the wish.

She picked up those crazy rubber gloves in Africa—that much I know. But Gran never did tell the whole story. Maybe there's more to it. Maybe there's some reason for the gloves to have some sort of freakish special abilities. Who am I to say the wish didn't come from those froufrou-ed dishwashing gloves that smelled like old tires?

I need to talk to Gran. Now.

"What?" asks Joules. "You want to try?"

"No." I motion toward her black T-shirt and my yellow one. "Switch tops with me."

"What? Forget it. I like this one."

"I have to go someplace and I don't want the photographers to follow. And give me your headband and sunglasses."

"Seriously? You're going to screw up my term if you miss class."

"Like you ever cared about that."

"I do! And anyway, I'm not changing tops . . ."

"You want your life back, Joules? Or would you

243

rather live out your life in dirty diapers and vomit?"

She looks around and motions for me to follow her to the little alcove where the custodian parks his truck. The place is covered on three sides and private enough, as long as no one happens along. There, she pulls off her top and motions for me to do the same. "Where are you going? I want to come."

"You can't. I can't get an absence right now. I have the Stanford interview soon and I cannot afford to have another strike against me. Besides, there's the paps."

Joules snorts and pulls the black T-shirt over her head. "*Paps.* I swear, Birch Tree, you are the uncoolest girl ever. Even in my body."

As I race down the hallway in my old shirt, she calls after me, "Aren't you going to tell me where you're going?"

"I'm going to see someone about a pair of ruby slippers."

chapter 18

Turns out I didn't need the disguise. I stayed within school grounds and exited onto the street from the gym building—way on the other side of campus from where the paparazzi were posted—and jogged along a short alleyway until I got to Harbor Boulevard.

Gran's apartment is almost alarmingly normal. She lives in one of these Snow White and the Seven Dwarfs cottages in town, complete with pretty white curtains in the window. She has flowers in her garden and a straw mat in front of a glossy blue front door. I don't know what would be more fitting for her—maybe an African baobab instead of the lemon tree, and a scattering of poisonous frogs instead of impatiens.

I knock on the door, and right away she flings it open. "Yes?"

"This is going to sound weird."

She squints at me. "Is this about my newspaper? Because I'm on the Internets now."

"No." I step closer. "Gran, it's me. Andrea."

"Excuse me?"

One of her neighbors, a woman carrying a baby boy, looks concerned and calls from her porch, "Are you okay over there?"

Gran waves that she's fine, which sort of annoys me. I mean, she doesn't know Joules at all. How does she know Joules isn't working with some gang of home invaders who are hiding in the bushes, about to pop out and storm the house? Gran says, "I think we'd better go inside."

Inside, the house is even more normal. The walls are white and the tiny foyer has a sensible gray mat for wiping your shoes and a sturdy bench so Gran can put on her sneakers "without falling over and breaking a hip like some kind of old wrinkly." She leads me into the living room and motions for me to sit on her long, striped sofa.

"I'm not sure I understand what you're saying."

"Gran, I know it's weird, but I'm Andrea."

She drops into a chair and examines me. "My granddaughter?"

I nod.

Her eyes, blinking confusedly, travel from my shoes, up my legs and torso to my face. "Andrea Birch?"

"Yes. It makes no sense but, see, I was really upset. I'd missed the model tryouts and getting the free jeans and Mom was mad at me and Cici and Sam took my lip gloss and then Michaela was in my room and I couldn't even talk to Will—"

"I don't understand. Who's Will?"

I sigh and look up at the ceiling. "Only the greatest guy who ever lived. So there I was, and Mom told me to do the dishes and, well, I just took off. I ran as far as the bridge where the trains go overhead and, you know, Joules's life looked so unbelievably good—I mean, she actually kissed him right there in front of me, and I did a really stupid thing. Gran, I wished we could switch lives. And now I have my Stanford interview coming up. So stupid! It's not like I thought . . ."

"Oh dear." Gran holds her hand up for me to stop so I do. "You really are Andrea."

"Yes! I am. And I'm stuck in Joules's body."

"Well," she says with a snort, "there are worse bodies to be stuck in."

"*Gran.*"

"Mine, for instance."

"Gran! Can we focus? Do you think the rubber gloves could have done this? Because I was wearing them at the time."

247

She leans back in her chair and folds her arms. "Of course it's because of the gloves. I bought them from a roadside fortune teller in Africa. She was doing psychic readings from a fairly dinged-up crystal ball."

I'm so relieved. Because if we know how the switch happened, we know how to make the switch unhappen. "Good. This is good."

Then my stomach drops. Because I have no freaking idea where they are.

"You have them with you, I assume," Gran says, dead certain I am not stupid enough to let them out of my sight.

Only I am that stupid. I mean, they have to be back at the bridge, right? When I woke up, I was in Joules's room and they were nowhere to be seen. Then again, I've been back to the bridge—twice— and there was absolutely no sign of them.

"No. Not actually with me."

"Andrea. I told you when I gave them to you— you have to take good care of them. Are you keeping them in a safe place?"

"Totally." I nod way too fast. "I . . . totally. I keep them in a totally safe place."

•

248

Crazy to check the top of the slope beneath the bridge. You'd think I'd have noticed something as eye-catching as feather- and rhinestone-covered gloves. But I check anyway. It doesn't seem possible anybody could have taken them—who would hang out here except for an idiot like me?

I try a quick wish when a train thunders overhead—no surprise when it doesn't work—and once the last railway car has passed, I start to work my way back and forth along the grassy area beside the bridge. It's not easy, the hill is made of dust and rocks and gopher holes, with long patchy grass and bushes that have been scorched by the sun into tumbleweeds about to break loose and roll across town. The whole time I pray I don't find a rattlesnake or a scorpion or a nest of hairy tarantulas.

Pill bugs I can handle. Tarantulas . . . not so much.

There was this foster kid who came to us just over a year ago. I can't remember his name but he was twelve years old and obsessed with spiders—I don't know why, maybe he was never allowed to wear a Spider-Man costume as a kid. You know how kids are; you hold something back from them too much and it's for sure going to fester.

Anyway, this kid totally spooked me about tarantulas. Said that, when frightened, they can jump five feet in any direction, just like that. Splat. Hairy spider on your face. And they bite, too. But they have no venom. Being bitten by a tarantula is no worse than being stung by a bee. But still. It's no bee, it's a massive hairy spider.

The thing about this kid—Christopher was his name—was he'd lived in and out of group homes his entire life. His parents checked out of parenthood when he was about three but not by choice. I don't know what happened to his dad but his mom wound up getting multiple sclerosis and could no longer take care of him. And here's the kicker: he had relatives but not one stepped up. I guess none of them answered the phone or something when it came time to place Christopher in proper care. That's the kind of thing that kills you, imagining a three-year-old with a sick mother and no one answers the phone.

Eventually, after he placed in the nationals for math—the kid was smart—some relative claimed him. An uncle living up in New Jersey all of a sudden missed him enough to take him in. He wasn't too excited about going there, though. He said "They don't have nearly as scary spiders on the east coast."

The roadside is a disappointment. I find exactly what a person might expect to find. Plenty of candy bar wrappers and empty cigarette and gum packs, a greasy McDonald's bag and broken beer bottles in a wide variety of colors—light brown, dark brown, green, clear. There's one of those tiny Lego figures which I almost take home for our Lego bin but leave for the ground squirrels to have some fun with, a twisted cloth—really filthy—that was probably someone's T-shirt that flew out the back of a pickup, and a greasy dead crow that's had its eyes pecked out but otherwise looks pretty fresh.

I find a piece of skinny plastic hose (stained with what could definitely be blood) that some serial killer probably dropped between victims, and more broken beer bottles. This patch of land really is the home of the wasted. You wouldn't want to wander around here without thick-soled shoes, that's for sure. Even with such a treasure trove at my feet, no sign of the gloves.

I cross beneath the bridge again and go check out the other side. This area must be way less popular than the first. Even though it's in the sun, there's no broken glass whatsoever and hardly a speck of garbage. Maybe one gum wrapper, but that might have come over here on the bottom of my shoe. It's weird; right away I notice there are fewer weeds here,

too. Like no one can stand this side of the bridge—
not even the dandelions. It is a bit steeper, so, okay,
maybe it's less popular as a get-drunk hangout. Or,
if you're a serial killer, you might have more worries over here when it comes to solid footing. And
I think—I stand up taller and push my face up into
the breeze—yes, I'm sure. It's the windy side of the
bridge. The side Dad would say "takes the brunt
of it."

I sit down for a minute and stare at the cars passing by, surprised by the number of black SUVs on
the road. Three pass me by in a span of about five
minutes. They're never going to catch the guy who
hit Michaela's parents. Plus, you've got to assume the
driver would have had the car fixed after. What kind
of idiot would he be to drive around in it right now
with a dented hood and broken windshield?

Without even the shelter of the few struggling
trees on the other side, I get hot fast. It's brutal. I feel
like my skin is blistering before my eyes. I'm sweating and, maybe because I skipped breakfast, maybe
because I forgot about Joules's caffeine addiction, I
feel like I could faint.

That's when I see it. Way over to my right, just
beneath the concrete barrier that separates someone's

yard from the busyness of Harbor Boulevard, a teeny,
tiny sparkle of light. I take off at a run and drop to
my knees when I see first one crazy, dust-covered
rubber glove, then, about ten feet away, the other.

Laughing, skipping in place, I pull them on and
stare at them in wonder. That's it. I have the answer
now. I can run beneath the bridge and change everything back. I can jump out of Joules's crummy life
and back into my own. I can sleep in my bed and
stop drinking coffee and tickle the Ks and get bossed
around by Mom. I can ask Dad about the weather
and tell Cici and Sam yes, I'd love to go jogging with
them.

I can call Gran and say, "*Pleasepleasepleasepleaseplease* don't bring me back any more gifts from any
more places you travel."

I can be me.

Still wearing the gloves, I crawl back up to the
base of the bridge and flop backward in relief as I
wait for a train. I have no idea if a train is necessary
or if rain is necessary or if all I need is the gloves.
I'm exhausted, I feel it now. People aren't meant to
switch bodies, switch worlds. It's too hard to catch
up, seventeen years into the trouble another person
has created for themselves. What I'll do when I'm me

again, I'll sleep for as long as I want. Just sleep and sleep and sleep.

Then I'll wake up and never covet someone else's life again.

The ground starts to rumble and I sit up, wrap my arms around my knees and stare at the gloves. Some of the rhinestones have fallen out—or maybe were pecked out by the same beast that swallowed the crow's eyes. I guess the glue didn't hold so well in the hot sun because many of the feathers are gone as well.

The train is closer now, the piercing whistle hurts my ears. A few more seconds and it thunders over my head, spraying me once again with grit.

I hold up the gloves, but before I make my wish, the feel of Will's leg over mine hits me. The touch of his fingers pushing hair off my face. The smell of his breath. I came so close. Closer than I'll ever come to kissing him again.

I took too much time. I should have rushed it. Kissed him before Joules appeared. I mean, he likes me, I can see it. He knows there's a difference now, he knows Joules has changed. It's the me in her he's attracted to.

As the train crashes overhead, I have an idea. The

gloves are mine again, to use as I please. What's the rush?

I could put them in a safe place and wait. Not for long. Just until I can experience that kiss.

It's why I made the wish in the first place, right? To live, just once, the kiss I saw in the music room. To turn my back on that wish coming true could anger the . . . the wish-granting gods. It could send the message that I'm toying with the universe. Playing games with life.

One kiss.

And then.

The rattle overhead fades as the last cars pass and, as quickly as it arrived, the train is gone. One rubber finger at a time, I pull off the gloves. I stare at them, lying in my lap, fake gemstones winking up at the sky. With no backpack or purse to stash them in, I'm not sure what to do. Tuck them in my shirt, maybe, and when I get to school, stuff them in Joules's locker. Then hide them in her backpack after school.

I hear footsteps to my left and glance up the road to see my own body, dressed in gym clothes, jogging along the sidewalk toward me. Joules.

"Andrea!" she shouts.

I have to ditch the gloves. Fast. I run back up to

the concrete wall and, using a rock, madly dig a small hole in the ground. Once the gloves are tucked safely into it, I cover them over with dirt.

Joules is scrabbling up the embankment beneath the bridge. Closer now, but not close enough to see what I'm up to. "Andie! Did you find any ruby slippers?"

The girl actually thinks I have access to some sort of sparkly red pumps plucked from the striped-stockinged hooves of some witch felled by a bungalow in Munchkinland. For the zillionth time, I wonder about Joules's grades. Either a whole lot of rocker swag is being passed around this school or she's one of those book-smart/life-stupid people you sometimes come across.

Leaving the gloves in the ground like this is dangerous. I might forget where they are. I reach for the first bit of trash I see—the serial killer's hose—and coil it overtop of the gloves' temporary burial site, then saunter back down the hill toward her, all disappointed-looking.

"Nope. It's officially a ruby slipper–free zone."

"The photographers are gone—the police chased them away from campus." She walks up to me, then leans over her knees as if exhausted. "So get my butt back to school and make sure Will stays in love with me. Okay?"

I sigh, all weary, and think about the kiss that needs to happen. "Okay, okay. I'll do my best."

●

On the way back, Joules whines about the magic slippers and I assure her I'll have them anytime now. And that she can relax in the knowledge that she'll be back to sharing her caffeinated body with boys in the bushes before too long. (Although who am I to talk? I hadn't been in her body two days before I got pretty busy in the bushes myself. Wait, strike that. Tried. I tried to get busy in the bushes.)

Joules was right about the paparazzi—they're gone. Unfortunately, so is Will. And he'll be out for the rest of the day—the soccer team left at lunchtime for some sort of tournament in Chino Hills, so there'll be no chance of my lips being anywhere near his anytime this afternoon.

Shane, on the other hand, is here. He sidles up to me at my locker between third and fourth periods. "Hey, Joules."

"Hi, Shane." I start to walk away.

"I was thinking maybe I should drive you home today. You know, because of the photographers. "

"Thanks. But I'm good. Will is driving me."

"Will's in Chino Hills. It's perfect timing. You swore you'd make time for us."

I'm angry at Joules. She never told me she made promises to Shane. I stare at him and wonder what she sees in him. I mean, he's cute in a dumb surfer kind of way, but he doesn't compare to Will. "There's an us?"

He nods, grinning. "Definitely."

"Well, there can't be. Not any more. I'm sorry, Shane. I'm trying to work things out with Will. You and me, us, can no longer happen."

This time he barks out a laugh. As I walk away, he calls, "Yeah, right!"

Nigel calls me just after the final bell rings to say photographers are still swarming the house and do I want one of the publicists to pick me up? Better to dash from car to front door, he says, than have to walk through them out on the road. But I have no interest in hanging with either Clara or Sue right now, so

I tell him no. I take side streets and cut through the running trail to avoid being spotted and make my way over to my old neighborhood. I cross State College and head up and over the hill to Highcliffe Court just to reassure myself my house and family are still there. Stupid, I know. But now that I have a way back to my life, I need to make sure I still have one.

It's a funny house, all on one storey, and it looks a lot shorter than it actually is inside because the dark brown roof slopes down low. There's this walled courtyard area in the front, just to the left of the walkway by the double doors. Other houses on the street have this same three-walled space but theirs is tiled and usually has a couple of chairs and a bistro table, as if the owners envisioned themselves lounging out there with coffee every morning. But in all my years living here, I've never once seen it happen.

I position myself next to the mailboxes in the center of the cul-de-sac and pretend I've dropped something in the bushes so I can stare at the house for a minute without making anyone suspicious. Eventually the front door opens and Brayden and his crappy friends walk out. They play basketball on the driveway for a while, but not like regular boys. These guys trip each other and laugh when someone's knee starts to bleed.

One jumps at the net and hangs, feet kicking beneath him as he tries to break the rim. Tomas whips the ball at Bray as hard as he can. At one point a fight breaks out and Tomas presses Dillon's face to the concrete. Just when I'm ready to stomp over there and break it up, the other guys haul Tomas off him and Tomas starts shoving them around instead.

How Mom doesn't see the evil in these guys just baffles me.

When they move their baboonery into the garage, probably in search of garden tools to use as weapons, I make my way back to the main road and call Sue to come get me. If I have to pass through a throng of ravenous photographers, I'd like to do it wrapped in a couple of tons of metal and a feisty publicist.

chapter 19

The police arrive at 12:48 a.m.

There's nothing scarier than wicked pounding on your front door at that time of night. You're either about to be robbed, or your neighbor is in the midst of being murdered and is hoping you'll be able to wrangle the blood-soaked machete out of the madman's grasp, or the police have arrived to ask, "Are you a Miss Joules Adams?" while twirling a pair of handcuffs on an index finger like a Frisbee.

In this case it's the third.

I stand there at the door yawning like a moron in Joules's dead soldier coat while they start firing questions at me about my whereabouts this evening. My whereabouts? Can't they see I've just crawled out of bed? Even as Joules Freaking Adams I can't have caused too much trouble while sleeping.

"I've been here the whole time," I say, pulling the

coat closed so the short cop behind the other two will stop looking at my knees. "Ask my . . ." I realize my mistake too late. There's a photographer across the street, I can see the flash. Nigel must not come to the door or . . .

"What's going on here?" Nigel booms as he wanders over in boxers and undershirt. "You're hassling my daughter in the middle of the night?" Behind him Sue races up (I *knew* she was sleeping with Nigel! She's wearing nothing but a man's pajama top and came out of his bedroom. Also, it makes me wonder about her—doesn't she have a cat she needs to go home and feed? Or at least a plant that needs water?). She ushers Nigel away from the door, away from the photographer's lens, and demands to know what they want from the Adams family at such an hour.

The cop with the cuffs says, "Break-in over on Highcliffe Court. We have a few questions for the young lady."

I move closer, heart thumping. "Which house?"

Nigel roars from behind, "My daughter has been here all night!"

Sue waves the cops inside and shuts the door. "It's okay, Nige. I'll do the talking."

"Which house?" I repeat. "Is everyone okay?"

The short cop who was looking at my knees

squints at Nigel. "Hey, didn't I read you were off in rehab somewhere?"

"He's back," Sue says with great authority. "Finished his stint and returned home quietly. But neither of you know that. Now, is there anything else you need from us? It is rather late."

"Which house was it?" I repeat. "Was anyone hurt? What happened?"

"We need to take the young lady down to the station for questioning."

"Based on?" says Sue.

"Based on witnesses who can place her in a position near the house several hours before the incident. Watching it."

My house. It was my house.

Nigel and Sue look at me. "You were there?"

"No. Well, yes, but it's not what you think." I turn to Shorty. "Will you please tell me if everyone is okay? Was anyone home at the time?"

They fire questions at me.

"How long have you been watching the place, Miss Adams?"

"Were you with the others this afternoon?"

"Have you any involvement in the other break-and-enters in recent weeks?"

I'm too stunned to answer. All I can think of is my

family being stormed, maybe even tied up, terrified, maybe worse. "Please tell me if everyone is okay! Are all the babies okay? Was anyone hurt?"

The mention of the babies sends them all into action. They don't use the cuffs, and they do allow me time to change into jeans, but they lead me toward the door, with Nigel in the background saying he'd hop in the car with me but for the photographers. That he has no choice but to wait at the house. That he'll get hold of his lawyer and send him to the station.

To be honest, Nigel not having it in him to accompany Joules when she's being led toward a squad car in the middle of the night, it kind of makes me sick for her.

Maybe I don't know everything when it comes to Nigel Adams.

Outside, the black of the night explodes with camera flashes. I blink as I climb into the police car and realize in horror that this episode is going to be on Perez Hilton by sunrise.

Joules. Is. Going. To. Kill. Me.

· · ·

Finally. Once I'm in the interrogation room—this tiny

gray cell with no windows and a glaring light over my head, where I sit on one side of a small table and a cop sits on the other—I find out what happened. My family was out, and someone gained entry through the side door by punching through the window and reaching in to undo the lock.

I'm so relieved no one was home I could pass out. "What was taken?"

"Not much," the cop says. "Took the mother's engagement ring from a dish by the sink and a big TV from the back room."

I feel sick when I think Mom's ring might be gone forever. Anyone who's lived in our house for a month knows the story about that ring. Even when they were dating, Dad knew Mom wasn't a shiny new jewelry kind of girl. New gold has no history, she told him. No emotional value. She'd always, since she was a little girl, loved her grandmother's engagement ring. It's nothing flashy, just a plain platinum band and a small round diamond.

When Dad was ready to propose to Mom, her grandmother had just died and left the ring to my Gran. Without telling Mom, Dad went to Gran and asked for the ring. He took it to a jeweler and had *Lise & Gary* inscribed on the inside. Mom cried when she saw it. And she only ever takes it off to wash dishes.

Anyway, doesn't much matter now. It's gone. And of course it was in the little dish by the sink. That's where Mom puts it when she has to wash dishes without gloves.

And guess who took the gloves?

Me.

"Perps knew just where to head," one cop says. "I mean, how many crooks would think to check the chipped dish where the SOS pad dries out? Most would ransack the bedroom."

Not when they've just spent the afternoon at that very house and probably saw the diamond ring sitting right there while Mom washed up Kaia and Kaylee's 4:30 bottles.

It was Bray's friends—Tomas, Dillon and Ace.

"You'll get off easier if you tell us who brought you into this."

"No one brought me into this. I am not 'in' this!'"

He leans back in his chair and smirks like he doesn't believe me for a second. "Uh-huh."

"I'm serious. And shouldn't I have a lawyer present? Or at least my dad?"

"You want them here? I'll make a phone call."

I think about it. No. I'd rather be on my own.

Besides, Nigel can't possibly leave the house. It could kill his career. "No. I'm a big girl."

"So the neighbor just happened to see you squatting behind a mailbox watching the place the very day it's busted into and I'm meant to believe you weren't involved?"

"Yes."

"Uh-huh."

"I'm serious." It's not like I can start telling him about magic gloves right now. That would only get me locked up in a psych facility. "I, well, this is kind of embarrassing."

He tries not to roll his eyes. "Believe me, I've heard it all."

I smile nervously. "I'm kind of, well, I have a crush on one of the boys who was playing basketball in the driveway."

He sighs hard and leans forward again, sips his coffee. "You willing to name the boys in the driveway?"

"I don't know. Like I said, I kind of like this one guy . . ."

"It's either that or we hold you tonight."

I pretend to wrestle with the idea of turning in my lover. He prods me a bit more, brings in a plateful of donuts and a small coffee in a paper cup to cure this Joules headache I'm developing. Then I spill it. "Ace Curzon. Dillon Gee. And Tomas Mendocino, he's the cute one."

The cop stands up. "You did a good thing here tonight, Joules." He sets his business card on the table in front of me. Officer Carl Beasley.

He goes out the door and I hear him say to someone, "Round up Ace Curzon, Dillon Gee and Tomas Mendocino and bring them in here, pronto."

When I'm alone, I whisper to no one, "This is all my fault."

·

Well, shock of the night. Or I guess I should say morning, since it's after two. Nigel, the man himself, is on his way to come get me. Well, not me, exactly, but his daughter. I'm so glad for Joules I could almost cry. Nigel called a few minutes ago to say his career isn't enough to keep him from his Jujube. He was actually on his way into the garage, into the Model T, no matter what the consequences. Sue, of course, would drive. And Sue, of course, had a plan that would keep him from torpedoing her carefully orchestrated Nigel Adams comeback. So he's been texting me for the last twenty minutes from beneath a blanket in the backseat.

I see Brayden sitting on the bench in a hallway. Which makes no sense, since his friends haven't even been brought in yet.

From the look on Bray's face, he's pretty surprised to see me, too. Here's my chance. Bray might not have any respect for Andrea Birch but he sure does think Joules Adams is cool. Maybe, just maybe, I can influence him enough to make sure my family is safe.

I sit down beside him and stretch my legs out in front of me, saying nothing for a while. When he starts to fidget and look around like he might leave, I say, "Whatcha doing here?"

"My house was busted into." He motions down the hall. "My, um, parents are here looking at suspects' photos or whatever."

I fight the urge to run down the hall and look for them. Must remain casual. Detached. Joules-like. "They're here? But what about the Ks?"

"My Gran came over." Bray squints at me. "But how do you know about Kaylee and Kaia?"

Huge error! I struggle to find a reasonable explanation. "No. It's . . . no, I don't. I just . . . Andrea mentioned them once. You're from Sunnyside, right?"

He blushes worse than I've ever seen and right away starts to fix his hair. "Yeah."

"What's your name? Byron? Brian?"

"Brayden."

I nod and pretend to process this. "Weird. I could have sworn it was Byron."

Out of the corner of my eye I see him puff air into his palm and sniff to make sure he doesn't have bad breath. "It's Bray, actually."

"Cool."

I let a minute pass. "I see you around school with your friends. Those guys are a bunch of losers. Why do you hang with them?"

He's shocked, no question. He probably thought a girl like Joules would approve of Tomas and his posse of idiots. "I don't know. They're around."

"Pretty lame reason."

"What's it to you?"

"It's nothing to me. Why would it be anything to me?" I kick at something that isn't there.

"What are you doing here anyway?" he says.

I miss our crazy family so much I can't see straight, I don't say. I'm actually not sure how to answer this. I can't give him the story I gave the police—that I have it bad for Tomas. I can't tell the truth. And I don't want him to think Joules Adams gets into trouble or he'll think it's the cool thing to do.

"Did you see all the photographers following me today?"

"Yeah. Who didn't?"

"I was just filing a report. One of them dinged Nigel's car."

"That's so cool."

"That his car got junked?"

"No, that Nigel Adams is your dad. He's, like, the greatest."

I think of Brayden's room back home. Of the Nigel poster on his door. The one on the wall behind his bed. We may fight, Bray may drive me out of my mind and insult my body on a regular basis, but he's basically a decent kid who's had a crappy life. He caught a break being sent to Mom because she loves him about as much as any natural mother could.

The way he's looking at me now, with such awe, it wouldn't take much to give this little guy the thrill of a lifetime. "You like Nigel?"

He reaches into the backpack at his feet and pulls out Nigel's CD. "What do *you* think?"

I take it from him and look it over. The designer

has airbrushed the rumpled bedding look off Nigel's face. I grin at Bray. "Want to get it signed?"

"Seriously?"

I stand up. "Follow me." I take him outside to where Sue and Nigel are about to pull into the driveway.

"He's here? I thought he was in, you know . . ."

I look around as if making sure we're alone, then bend down to whisper in Bray's ear. "Can you keep a secret?"

The kid seriously looks like he might burst. "Yes."

"You'll be the only one outside of the family who knows it. So if it leaks I'll know exactly who to blame."

"I swear. I won't say anything."

I bend down to whisper in his ear. "He's been home the whole time."

Bray looks shocked.

"Swear you won't tell."

"I won't."

"Good. Because only you and his family knows. Only really close people."

The look on Bray's face at being told he's practically family is priceless. An upside-down smile crosses his face and he stands about six inches taller.

Just then the Model T pulls up and Sue leans over

to crank open the passenger-side window. Nigel's head pops up from beneath a blanket in the back. He grins when he sees Bray holding his CD. "You want that signed, mate?"

Bray's jaw drops. He can't even speak as he hands over the case with shaking hands. Nigel signs and passes it back to him. "Stay cool, dude."

Bray nods. "Yeah. Thanks!"

As I climb into the front seat, I shake a finger out the window at Brayden. "Remember. Get yourself some better friends and you'll be a half-decent kid."

Still stunned, still standing tall, he watches the car pull away and waves. I turn around and give Nigel a smile. "Hey, Dad? Thanks for coming."

Nigel leans forward and presses a kiss to my forehead.

chapter 20

It's Will's idea to meet in the cabana out behind the garage just after I get back to Joules's place. It's late, very late, nearly three in the morning, but he insists. Says that after a depressing day of losing to the Chino Wildcats, after being rudely interrupted in the bushes earlier, that he needs to see me. And that he has something to say to me.

I should go straight back to the bridge. I could have stopped the break-and-enter if I'd made the wish earlier this morning, and I'm crazy with guilt and determined to right everything and everyone I've wronged.

But I'm tired after the interrogation. I promise myself to head back there first thing in the morning. Even though Sue and Nigel are still up, I tell Will to come on over.

A girl like Andrea Birch doesn't get an invitation from Will Sherwood every day. What possible harm can come from waiting a few more hours at this point?

I, of course, have a very short commute from my bedroom window. I go around behind the pool so Nige and Sue won't see me. They're in the living room, lying on the couch pretending to watch something on TV. Sue's hand is up Nigel's shirt.

What I didn't count on was the cabana door being locked. I have absolutely no idea where to find a key, and asking Nigel is not an option. So I sit on the patio, leaning against the door, and wrap my sweater around my knees as I wait for Will.

The moon is huge tonight. Not quite full but in another night or so it will be. It seems hung so low I could reach up and touch it. Pluck it from the sky and use it as a pillow. Aware that I might not be as hidden as I think, I shift farther into the shadows.

He doesn't take long—he appears from behind a row of cypress trees on the far side of the yard, with a big grin on his face. Without a word, he pulls me to my feet and rattles the cabana door. "Locked?"

I shrug. "I don't have a key."

He glances around the backyard and nods toward the pool, which is steaming in the cool night air. "Skinny-dip?"

I point to the window, through which we can see Sue climbing onto Nigel's lap. "Too risky," I say. I try the rear door to the garage and it opens. "In here."

The moonlight pouring in from the garage window is bright enough that we can see fairly well. I pull a tarp off a shelf and spread it on the floor in a darkish corner, crawl across it and wait.

But Will is standing agape in front of the Model T. He runs his hands along the door. "Are you kidding me? Nige has a Flivver?" The window is rolled down and he touches the cracked leather seat the way I wish he would touch me. "This is gorgeous. I mean, seriously great." He looks over my way. "Have you been in it?"

I nod. "The other night. We took it out to Balboa Island. Also . . ." It would be too complicated to explain I just had a ride home in it half an hour ago. "Also another time."

"Well, tell the old man if he ever needs anyone to wash it, wax it, love it . . . I am so willing."

"Good to know." I lean back on my elbows. "Will, maybe we should . . . it's getting pretty late."

He grins again but doesn't move. "Come here, Joules. I want to kiss you in the light where I can see you."

I get up, walk over to him and pause, not sure if I should take him in my arms like I want to, or wait and see what he does. Every fiber of my being wants to get closer to him, to become part of him even, but the Andrea Birch in me makes me hesitate.

He tugs on my crossed arms and pulls me in. "Should we check under the car in case Andrea is about to jump out and climb between us?"

I'm horrified—once I switch back I'll have to get used to him thinking I'm some kind of insane stalker chick—but smile. "She's not so bad."

He nods toward a tarped vehicle. "How freaky would it be if she popped out from beneath that blanket right now?"

"She wouldn't. Today was weird. I think she wasn't feeling well or something."

"What's under that blanket anyway? Don't tell me it's an even nicer antique car."

I should know what cars we own. A daughter would have to be an idiot not to know. "It's been a long day. I forget the make."

He walks across the garage and pulls back the tarp to reveal a huge fat wheel of a truck. Then, with a mighty heave, he uncovers the entire front end. The dented front end with smashed windshield.

It's not a truck. It's an SUV.

Black.

With a damaged front end.

Exactly what the police are looking for.

Will is thinking the same thing. I can see it in his eyes. We both look from the dented bumper to each other. Horrified. Frightened. Stunned stupid.

The truth is pretty hard to ignore, but each of us knows a different version of it. To Will, Nigel Adams is the Disneyland hit-and-run driver. To me, he ran down Michaela's parents and left a four-year-old girl to weep alone in the street.

Just then there is a grunt from the doorway to the house and the lights flick on overhead.

Nigel himself stands in the doorway. Without saying a word, he crosses the floor and stands between us, arms crossed over his chest as he surveys the damaged vehicle. I watch his eyes travel from the small scrape on the bumper to the larger indentation on the hood to the shattered glass with the distinct impression of a human head at its center.

It's as if a storm cloud passes over Nigel's face. Slowly, methodically, as if trying to prevent further destruction, he lowers the tarp back over the front of the SUV and says in a quiet voice, "Go home, Will. And Joules, get inside the house. Now."

chapter 21

Will's face, as he passes through the garage door, is a mix of disgust for Nigel and concern for me. He pauses, willing, I think, to brave Nigel's wrath if I ask him to stay; wondering if I'm at all worried for my own safety. And I am, believe me, but I nod toward the backyard to let him know it's fine for him to leave. He lifts his hand in a half-wave and disappears into the shadows.

Now it's just me and Nigel.

It's not a storm The Weather Show can track. Nigel is eerily quiet as he leads me back to the house and locks the door. To be honest, now I'm terrified. I mean, what do I really know about this man? He might wear an apron to protect his rocker jeans while he bakes croissants, and he might do dorky things to prove to his daughter he really is worthy of her love and respect. He might have a great croaker of a cigarette-scarred voice that makes millions of girls swoon all across the globe, and he might have publicists forgetting to go home and feed their parakeets, but I know very little of what to expect here. One thing I know for sure: he fooled me good.

I'd never have thought he was capable of this. Plowing into a pair of tourists and taking off, then burying the evidence beneath a tarp in his garage. I came into this house, saw the sad father in him surface and formed my opinion of him based on that and his generous nature.

The question is: what else is Nigel Adams capable of?

In the living room he turns to face me. His arms hang by his sides and one fist tightens into a ball. He won't hit Joules. Surely she'd have warned me if things were bad like that.

I take a step backward. He's standing between me and the door. I can't run, I'd never make it past him. Besides, heading back through the yard isn't an option, he'd catch me before I got the locked door open.

I have Joules's cellphone. I could lock myself in her room and call 911.

He blinks, and right away I feel like an idiot. This

is Nigel. He adores his daughter. There's no freaking way he would harm her—he lives for her love.

Still, I can't be in the same house with the man who destroyed Michaela's life and doesn't have the guts to face up to it. So I do something I know will absolutely crush him. I brush past, head out the back door and through the neighbor's shadowy yard, and just keep walking.

•

The hills aren't safe at night. In the dark, navigating the twisty, turny, rocky paths would be dangerous, and too scary for a girl like me to attempt. Out here there are probably rattlesnakes and lizards. There are certainly coyotes, and once, a couple of years ago, there were reports of some kind of big cat—a cougar, I think. It had been snacking on neighborhood pets went the story. I don't know anyone who actually saw it, but I didn't venture out much by myself just the same.

But tonight is different. The moon isn't looming quite as large now but it still has the land lit up as if dawn were about to break. Which, seeing that it's nearly 4 a.m., I guess it is. I head out on a narrow trail across the grassy slope with plans to cross the oil fields below and, well, I don't have much of a plan beyond that.

It was stupid, storming out so fast. My T-shirt and jeans are too thin to offer any warmth against the cool night air. If I'd been thinking straight, I'd have at least popped into Joules's room for the dead soldier coat. It would have served two purposes: keeping out the damp air and offering a sturdy layer between me and the dry grass and weeds I will eventually curl up on if I ever give in to the bone-weariness that has penetrated Joules's body.

Joules. All this time I thought she was such a spoiled little witch. I thought that I—who've known Nigel, what, a couple of days?—with my sensitive upbringing and experience dealing with broken souls, was better able to see his character than his own daughter.

I'll admit now, it's possible, likely even, that Joules knows more about her father than I know.

Equally possible and likely is that I know almost nothing about him at all.

I reach into my back pocket and finger the policeman's card. Officer Carl Beasley. The right thing to do would be to flip open Joules's phone and make that call. A mother and a father are lying in hospital beds, without their daughter, because of Nigel. It isn't right that his PR babes shush this one up as well. Nigel must be made to pay for what he's done.

Taking hold of a branch from a dead bush, I pick my way down a small, dusty overhang, then stumble at the bottom and sit there a moment, overwhelmed by exhaustion. I need to stop. Stop thinking. Stop feeling. Stop caring. If I had the energy, I would run back to the wall beside the bridge right now and dig up the gloves. If I had the energy, I would wish myself out of this situation and back into the life I would now kill to be part of.

But I don't have the energy. I'm depleted.

The wind picks up, and everywhere around me leaves and grass rustle. At least I hope it's the wind. It could be the cougar. The thought of meeting the big cat face to face drives me forward. I walk on.

Naturally, State College is empty when I happen upon it. Who in their right mind would be headed anywhere at four in the morning? I trudge across the road and take the sidewalk to the top of the hill. As if propelled by remote control, I turn right on Mountain Ridge and wind down to the place where I feel safer than any other on earth—my parents' house.

The side door to the garage is, as usual, unlocked.

Even after the break-in no one has thought to bolt it shut at night. There's no window in this garage, no moonlight to help me find my way around, but I don't need it. I pull two rolled sleeping bags down from Dad's tidy shelving unit and spread them out in the corner; the downy fabric isn't nearly thick enough to protect me from the concrete floor below but I'm too tired to care. I curl in a ball and cover myself with the second, unzipped bag. I'm home.

Sort of.

Before I drift off, I decide this: I can't go back for the gloves just yet. Nigel must turn himself in, and his daughter must be the one to encourage it. I cannot trust Joules to enforce a thing like that. And if I call the police as her, Nigel will be devastated. No. He must do the dirty deed himself. It will elevate him in his daughter's eyes, that he at least had the decency to own up to his crime rather than beg Clara and Sue to get creative.

I'll go back and insist. I'll talk about responsibility and atonement and being able to walk about this earth with your head held high. Coming from Joules, the message might penetrate. To please his daughter, he might follow through.

But not now.

Fully aware that Nigel must be inside-out with worry for Joules, feeling guilt but not enough guilt to tempt me off the cement floor and back into his house, I sleep.

•

I'm awakened by the feel of someone staring down at me. My eyes fly open to see Dad's face—my dad, Gary's, face. He's squatting down beside me with toast wrapped in paper towel and a cup of steaming coffee. Without a word, he holds it out to me.

I sit up and take his offerings. "Thanks."

"You could have knocked on our door," he says with a sad wink. "If nothing else, my wife and I know troubled kids."

"I'm not troubled."

He nods and hands me a card—Child Services, Lilith Parcelle, the woman who comes by the house to check on the kids. The flowered pants lady. "Just in case you ever are . . . troubled." With that, he stands up and heads to the door. Looks back. "I'll leave the garage unlocked, but if you have real problems you call that number."

"I don't. But thanks."

And he's gone.

After rolling up the sleeping bags and parking them on the shelf, I take my coffee and toast and head back to Skyline, to what will be the biggest confrontation of Joules's life.

Or is it mine?

chapter 22

The Panel of Undoers awaits me in the kitchen—
Sue and her perky sidekick, Clara, Nigel and his
agent, plus the Hendridge boys, who may or may not
be his managers. From the looks of the wine bottles
on the island, the pizza boxes, the empty coffee cups
and the state of Nigel's hair—standing on end—it's
been a long night.

Nigel sees me first. He stands, crosses the room
and takes me into his arms, whispering "Jujube" into
my hair, kissing the top of my head over and over.

I'd be lying if I said I didn't feel guilty. Or if I
said I thought Nigel was a terrible person. He isn't.
He's scared and flawed and spoiled and childish. He
might understand right from wrong but no one in his
inner circle lets him suffer the natural consequences
that arise from poor life choices. All he knows is the
way out.

"You don't have to tell me where you were," he says. "That you're here now is all I need."

The way out.

"Dad. We have to talk."

"Nige has a terrific plan for the two of you today," Sue says, spreading a few brochures across the island. I look closer to see they're from car dealerships— fancy car dealerships. "He's been thinking it might be time for you to get your own set of wheels, and I've booked you appointments at three different dealerships."

Perky sidekick grins. "I wish *my* dad had surprised *me* with something like this when I was seventeen."

So this is the plan. Appease me through distraction. A nice, subtle, pearl-black convertible bribe to keep my mouth shut.

I look at Nigel. "Nigel. We can't just move forward like nothing has happened. It isn't right. That couple is suffering because . . . well, because of you and—"

Nigel squeezes my shoulder. "Sweetness, let's not put a damper on the day. You let us work that out— we're the adults here."

No, I want to say. *You aren't the adults. Adults don't try to buy their way out of trouble. Adults avoid it in the first place and confront it with honesty if it happens.* "I just think we need to call and report what—"

A bell goes off and Nigel opens the oven. More croissants. "Let's have ourselves some breakfast and talk about it in the Model T, okay? Sue here will call the school to report your absence, I'll hide away in the back, and once we get far enough away from the leeches with the cameras we'll have a day to ourselves. Drive up the coast or something."

"No. I'm not going. You need to make the call. If you ever want me to respect you, you need to stop slinking around like this when you mess up, or—here's a wild thought—stop drinking and driving in the first place! This world isn't a . . . a playground for you. It's not your right to just plow through it without ever once suffering a consequence. Don't you get that?"

You should see Nigel's face. It nearly folds over itself with pain. Like I've punched him so hard I've shattered all the bones that shape it.

Sue stands up. "Now, now, that's enough."

I knock her arm off my shoulder. "You have to convince him," I say to her. "He can't just go on like this. If he doesn't do anything about it, I will."

The manager says, "Let's settle down, Julie. This

is not tenth-grade ethics class, this is real life—"

"It's Joules," I spit. "*Joules.*"

It's as if I haven't even spoken.

"You can't just walk into a police station and make some outlandish claim about a man like Nigel Adams because you're ticked off," he says. "You need to have proof. It's a case of 'he said, she said', and your dad has a rock-solid alibi for that night."

I can't take it any more. I stomp out to the garage and fling the door open. There, where the tarp-covered SUV was just six or seven hours ago, is nothing but a folded piece of canvas. The car is gone.

I stand there a moment, stunned.

A few years back, I had a foster sister for less than ten months. She was this tall girl with bad skin who slumped down to appear the size of everyone else but, of course, failed and wound up looking like a girl who hated her height. It made me crazy, all that hunching. It was as if she wanted to disappear. Tatiana was her name. Thirteen years old but taller than Dad. She was only with us temporarily, she kept saying. Because the aunt who took care of her— nobody knew where her actual mother was—needed surgery. Once her aunt was better, she'd be gone. But the surgery came and went and the aunt had all these excuses. Eventually Mom found out there was no surgery at all, just a new boyfriend who didn't want a kid hanging around and an aunt who said she'd done more than her share already.

Nice family.

There's something about the randomness of who we're born to. As lousy as things seem when you really examine them, as random as our births all appear, there may be a sense of order I've missed.

It's called love.

People like Lise and Gary Birch are here to make sense of what would otherwise be sheer madness. They're part of the system, these generous people who open their doors to soothe and care for the ones who haven't been so lucky. They, and others like them, are here to make sense of all the dreck, even if their influence is only temporary. They're here to undo the damage inflicted by people who should never have been allowed to have children in the first place.

Their own daughter was too selfish to really see it. And just might have been the luckiest one of all.

I pull Joules's phone from my pocket. She picks up right away. I can hear the Ks gurgling in the background.

"Meet me at the bridge," I say. "Now."

chapter 23

The train didn't work. The rainstorm didn't work. But neither of those things were sold to my grandma by the crystal ball witch of Africa.

Joules doesn't look pleased as I make my way up the gravelly slope beneath the bridge.

"Your mom made pancakes." She picks up a handful of pebbles and watches them trickle between her fingers. "You couldn't have waited another half hour? I'm starved."

"Let's just get this done. One more hour in your life might just finish me off."

She scoffs. "Yeah. Like yours is so great. What's with those white sandals your mother wears? She looks like a fifty-year-old baby."

I shove my hands into my back pockets because I'm afraid I might slap her. "Let's not get into the differences in our bloodlines right now, okay?"

292

"And why don't you show her how to shave her legs? I can't even eat in that house. Oh, and I found an ad for the overseas foster kids. I left it on her kitchen table as a hint."

Yesterday, I'd have jumped into the whole "Why do you treat Nigel like garbage?" thing. Today I know better. That Nigel thinks he can sanitize his daughter's image of himself by spiking her coffee and making croissants. It's so pathetic, so sad, I can hardly stand it.

"Yeah, well. I refuse to discuss who has the better parent. I'm not sure there's any contest."

She eyes me closely. "Does this mean you're over the whole I-don't-fawn-enough-over-my-rock-star-dad thing?"

"Yes."

"I'm not the bitch you make me out to be, you know. I used to be a better daughter." She shrugs. "There was even a time I bought into the whole rocker lifestyle. Not any more."

"Believe me, I—"

"My dad isn't as generous as he seems."

Is it possible she knows? I decide to test her. "Well, he does give to that family—Tyler Glass's family. That's pretty generous."

"Wake up. He doesn't do that from the sweetness of his heart. He does it out of guilt."

I could throw up from where I think this is headed and hope this is not headed. Nigel couldn't have. He *couldn't* have.

She moves closer. "My father has a problem. He drinks. He drives."

"I know."

"Yeah? Well, did you know this? Nigel killed Tyler Glass."

Behind me traffic roars past. I don't look away from Joules but I can hear one of the cars has a muffler dragging on the ground. I can't believe it. I mean, the news reports have speculated it could be the same driver, but this . . . that he actually killed a child?

"Oh God."

"What a guy, right? What a freakishly fantastic guy."

"Nigel killed Tyler Glass? He really did?"

"Are you deaf?"

I don't answer.

She stares at me. "And then there's more recent developments. Have you been in the garage lately? Have you peeked beneath the tarp?"

I drop to the ground beside her and let out a long

breath. "He caught me looking. Sorry. He knows you know about the Disneyland couple."

She shrugs. "Whatever. He knows I know about Tyler, too."

"How?"

She looks at me as if I'm an idiot. "I was in the SUV with him. Screaming at him to stop. Go back. But he was drinking champagne. The SUV was full of evidence. He said he'd make it up to them. He said he'd write a song for Tyler. That single was never for me."

All the money he donates publicly to that family. "Rockabye." All out of guilt.

We're quiet a moment. The modest house Joules and Nigel live in—it makes more sense now. He forks over most of his paychecks to undo the damage he inflicts upon the world.

I don't have the heart to tell her that the little girl who's been sleeping in my bedroom next to her is the Disneyland couple's child. Instead, I stand up and motion toward the cement sound barrier. "The ruby slippers are over there."

"Andie?"

Even at such a moment, I like the way that sounds. "Yeah?"

"I'm not sure I want to go back." She stares up at me, a tear inching down her cheek. "Isn't that crazy? I don't know if I want my stupid life back. Maybe I want yours."

I pull her up to standing and laugh sadly. "If I'd heard that a few days ago, I'd have been shocked."

"Want to be more shocked? I wished for this too."

Too tired to tell her I know this already, I try to arrange my face into a surprised expression.

"That night I was with Will and you were here. I saw the way he spoke with you in the music room earlier that day. It was so different from the way he treats me, and I was jealous. I wanted to be you and have him talk to me all respectful like that. Plus, the big family. You seemed to have it all."

I did have it all. I just didn't know it.

"So, it's not all your fault," she says, "this wish thing."

I nod but say nothing.

"He's different with you. Even when you're me. It's so obvious when I see you two together. Will and I . . . we're wrong."

It's true. The way he is with Joules might look intense from the outside, but it's more about admiring her physical self. With me, I don't know, with me there's something deeper. But I'd never tell Joules that.

"No," I say. "Not wrong."

She shakes her head and looks away. "It's okay. What am I going to do? Force him to like me more? I can't do that. Anyway, whatever. There's always Shane in the bushes, right?"

I'm not sure if she's joking or not, but when she laughs I join her. "He is kind of cute."

She nods. "Right? I've always been a sucker for the surfer dude look."

A blue jay cries out from the trees to our right and we both look. It flies toward us, but the bridge blocks it out as it passes overhead.

"Hey." Joules stares at me. "I got Michaela to laugh this morning. We were brushing our teeth together in the bathroom and I was goofing around. My toothbrush fell in the toilet. She looked worried for a second, then when she saw I wasn't upset, she totally started to giggle." She smiles. "It was good to see."

Joules's previously impenetrable shell is starting to crack. The fosters are getting to her.

"Pretty wild for both of us," she adds. "To see how the other one really lives. My life isn't quite what you read about in the tabloids, is it."

Still holding her wrists, I say, "You won't be alone with it all any more. I'm tough to get rid of."

We walk across the grass in silence. At the wall, I drop to my knees and fling the serial killer hose out of the way, then start to dig.

"They're not really shoes we're digging up, are they?"

It hasn't rained since the other day and the ground is unforgiving. "They're rubber gloves." I can feel dirt packing itself deep beneath my fingernails. Joules bends down to help. The digging is tough, so we both reach for sharp rocks, sharp sticks to help penetrate the earth. Eventually we hit red clay.

I never saw red clay the first time, which means we've dug too deep. I look around to check my landmarks. The crack in the cement wall. The dead bush about a foot to the left. This is definitely the place.

So where are the gloves?

With panic blocking my throat, I look at Joules. "They're not here."

"What do you mean they're not here?"

"I mean they're not here! I buried them right here to keep them safe and . . ." I stand up and look around wildly, my chest heaving up and down. "Somebody took them. Somebody dug them up and took them!"

"You mean we have no way to wish back?"

I stomp along the wall to see if some animal dug them up, thinking they were food, and left them all chewed up among the trash. Nothing.

"Andie! Where are the gloves?"

"I don't know, okay?" I wander around the entire plot of weeds and grass to find zero evidence of Gran's magic gloves. But there's not a feather, not a rhinestone, not so much as a chewed-up piece of black rubber. I go back to the hole and dig wider around the mouth of it.

There's no mistaking it. The gloves are gone.

chapter 24

We've combed this area three times. We've crossed beneath the bridge and searched the littered side twice. We've checked out the train tracks, and I've even scaled the cement wall to have a look in the yards nearby.

All we've come up with is a whole lot of nothing.

Joules, who just ten minutes ago was saying she didn't want to go back, is staring out into traffic, crying. I'm numb. It was one thing to talk about not switching back when we still had hope. Without hope, the prospect of remaining each other is terrifying.

"How could you think burying them and leaving them behind was safe?" she whispers.

I can't answer.

"And what was your reason?"

I *really* can't answer that one.

"Seriously. You couldn't have brought them back

to my house and put them under the bed or something? What were you thinking?"

"I don't know."

She flops her hands in the dirt. "So this is it. For
the rest of my life I walk around as . . ." she waves
her arms angrily above her head, "Andrea Birch?"
Her voice rises in pitch. "I mean, this is it? This is
really *it?*"

"Don't panic. We can still find them."

"Yeah? How? Some person came along and dug
them up. Took them. How are we ever going to
figure out who?"

"I don't know, okay? Let me think."

She wraps her arms around her knees and starts
to rock.

"*Ohmygodohmygodohmygodohmygodohmygod*. This
isn't happening. This totally isn't happening."

I put my arm around her and finally let myself cry.
"I know. I know. Joules, I'm so sorry."

She leans her head against my shoulder and starts to
sob with me. A bearded guy walking past stops, moves
closer to ask if we're okay. Neither of us has the energy
to answer, but he waits. When we're both spent, when
we have no more tears left to cry, we wipe our filthy
faces and look up at the guy. Joules speaks first.

"It's okay. My friend's cat just died is all." She puts her arms around me. "She really loved that stupid cat."

After he moves on, Joules surprises me by offering up a sad smile. "It's okay. We'll keep looking for the gloves. We'll find them. Nigel always says there's a scratch . . ."

"For every itch," I say.

"They're not gone. They're out there, right?"

They are. Somewhere. But looking for a couple of pieces of scrap rubber isn't like looking for a missing grandmother or a lost dog. You can't inform the police or ask your local radio station to air your plea.

The gloves were probably dug up by a couple of kids who had a quick laugh and stuffed them in a garbage can. Or the serial killer with the stained hose—maybe he's tired of scrubbing dried blood from his cuticles and has determined to cover his hands next time around. Kids or killers, it doesn't really matter.

We're never going to find those gloves.

Wait.

Gran.

Maybe there was another pair! Maybe she can find the roadside fortune teller and buy another pair! I pull out Joules's cellphone and start to dial.

switch

"What are you doing?" she asks, scooting closer.

I hold a finger to my mouth to shush her as Gran picks up.

"Hello?"

"Gran. It's Andrea."

She's silent for a moment. "Which Andrea?"

"I'm still Joules. Listen, Gran. I need another pair of those gloves."

"Another pair?"

"You can get more, right? I mean, they couldn't have been the only pair. I was thinking we could call her. The witch. Give her a credit card number and have her mail them or something. Was there another pair?"

"All she had on her table were the one pair of gloves and her crystal ball. There was no other pair."

My throat starts to tighten. "But...maybe if we call... she could make us another pair."

"She was a dust-covered soothsayer in the plains of Africa. She didn't hand out business cards. I doubt she even has a phone. What's going on here, Andrea? Don't tell me you've lost the gloves. I told you to take very special care not to lose them . . ."

I drop the phone into my lap.

Joules stares at me, her cheek scratched and her

303

face smeared with dirt. She could be five years old, the way she's looking at me to fix her world. "It's going to be okay, though. We'll find them one day, right?"

I push my chin up in the air and take a deep breath. "We'll totally find them."

chapter 25

What choice do we have? We dust ourselves off. We walk to Pizza Hut and splash water on our dirt-smeared faces in the bathroom. I buy us a Coke and a slice with Nigel's money. Then we go to school and sit in each other's chairs at each other's desks in each other's classes.

Only now it's different. Now I walk around in Joules's life knowing this may be it for me. No more play-acting. The assignment on the board in Algebra is *my* assignment. The graffiti-ed binder in the bag at my feet is *my* binder. The mop-haired boy across the room who keeps looking at me is *my* boyfriend.

What a difference a week makes.

The Stanford interview no longer matters. Joules has nine days to decide what she wants to do as Andrea Birch.

Will keeps silently raising his eyebrows as if to ask

if everything's all right. It isn't but I nod anyway. He winks, which is probably supposed to assure me he's on my side. But the wink hits me harder than that. More than anything right now, I want to lay my cheek on his shoulder. Listen to his heartbeat.

I take my pen in both hands and snap it in half. "Ms. Wigg?" I hold up an inky hand. "My pen leaked. May I go wash my hands?"

She nods and turns back to the blackboard where she writes out tonight's homework assignment.

Out in the hall, I lean against the iron railing and wait. A few minutes later, he's standing beside me. "You okay?"

Holding my stained hands away from his shirt, I wrap my arms around his neck. "Yes. No."

"What can I do?"

I shake my head, nothing. "Remember you said I was a different person before?"

He nods.

"And I said, no, I wasn't?"

"Yeah."

"I lied. I'm not the girl you used to date. Not even close. And I may never be again. Are you okay with that?"

He grins. "Sure."

"You think I'm kidding, right? Exaggerating?"

"No. You mean you've changed. I get it."

"I'm not sure you realize how much I've changed. I mean, in some ways I haven't changed one single solitary bit. I'm still the me I always was. And always will be. That part of me can learn and grow but never really change, you know? But in other ways," I hold up my hand, Joules's hand, "I'm completely someone else. As in physically. I am not myself, physically. Not even close. Not even kind of close. I'm wa-a-ay off in another state of being, this freakishly impossible state of being . . ."

Will looks confused. "You don't sound like Joules right now."

My babbling. Of course! "Right! Who do I sound like?"

"I'm not sure I should say."

"Say."

"You might not like it."

"Please say."

"You sound like Andrea Birch."

I smile, relieved. "I am Andrea Birch, Will. It's me in here." I touch my chest. "It's Andrea." I remember what Joules called me at the bridge. "Andie."

He stares at me as if waiting for some sort of punch line to this joke. "You're telling me *you're* Andrea?"

"It makes no sense, I know. But there was a wish.

My fault and Joules's fault. We both wished it. And it happened."

"You switched bodies? Lives?"

"Yes."

His eyes dart to the right and I watch as he tries to decide what to make of this information. Squinting, he looks at me again. "That's not possible."

"I know."

"As in, it's completely impossible."

"Right? That's what I thought. And yet." I wave toward Joules's body. "Maybe we can switch back, maybe we can't. Right now it isn't looking good."

He says nothing.

"But I want you to know who you're kissing."

"Who am I kissing?"

I rise up on my tiptoes and kiss him just to the right of his mouth. Light-headed from the warmth of his skin, I let my lips graze his as I whisper, "Me."

That's when my boyfriend kisses me back.

chapter 26

When some sort of shocking gossip floods a school it's impossible to ignore. It's like a swarm of bees—you feel the air buzzing long before you see the huddled bodies, hear the excited drone. By lunchtime, Sunnyside High is undulating with news, and it isn't until I reach the cafeteria that I realize it's me people are talking about.

A group of girls stop whispering as I enter, and even the lunch ladies avert their eyes as I grab a tray and get in line. The entire place falls silent. I ask, and am given, the lunch special—hamburger and fries with a dollop of milky cole slaw on the side. As if nothing is bothering me, I slide my tray along the rails behind the other kids—most of whom are stealing glances at me along the way—and pull a lunch ticket out of my pocket.

Bess, the heavyset woman at the cash who used to

tell me about her grandkids back when I was Andrea, gives me a warm smile as she takes my ticket. Then, as I lift my tray, she reaches out to pat my hand and says, "It's okay, pet. We're all of us just human."

I set my tray down again. "What's going on?"

She reaches for a folded newspaper and places it on the counter. The headline reads "Hit-and-Run Rock Star." There's Nigel's mug shot from the other night, and right beside it, that photo of the Disneyland couple in side-by-side hospital beds.

Nigel's been arrested.

It had to happen. I know that. But imagining him sitting in that kitchen with the PR girls, in his holey pajamas with his dirty hair; the thought of his stricken face when I called him a drunk, because all he really wants in life is Joules's—my—approval; now, the thought of him in jail, all of it makes me want to throw up.

Why does he have to be so self-destructive?

Bess says, "It's his life, honey. Not yours. We are not our families, you just remember that." She sounds like Mom. I have to stop myself from curling up in her lap like an old cat. Or a new foster child.

There is a lineup behind me, I'm taking too long. Even though I'd love to read the article, there's no

switch

way I'll do it in front of all these people. I lean closer to Bess. "How did it happen? How did they find out?"

Bess blinks at me. "Your dad did the right thing, sweetheart. He turned himself in."

I start to nod. Slowly at first, then quicker and quicker until I am backing away from my food and toward the door.

Outside, with a tight smile on my face, I break into a run and head home. To Skyline Drive, to Sue, who can hopefully tell me where to find him. Nigel. I need to tell him something.

I need to tell him I'm proud of him.

chapter 27

I was wrong about the inside of my house. My real
house. It does have a smell.

I stand in the foyer after not having lived here for
two weeks and inhale deeply. Here's the thing—it
takes a bit of distance for you to be able to detect it
in your own home. And it's not what I would have
thought. If asked what 8407 Highcliffe Court smells
like I might have said fabric softener or Mom's veggie
chili. But it's nothing like that. This house, the Birch
house, smells like kids. Dirty sneakers and boys who
have just come in after rolling in the grass and the
double stroller littered with dry Cheerios that's parked
by the front door.

It smells like a house that isn't pretending to be
anything other than what it is. A safe place that lets
kids step away from whatever garbage they've lived
through and finally, finally be kids.

Not that it's my house any more.

Over the weekend, Nigel was charged with reckless driving and leaving the scene of an accident. And since he confessed to killing Tyler Glass, he was also charged with vehicular manslaughter. That he was sipping champagne in the car didn't help. The judge went soft on him because he turned himself in and made the prosecutor's job that much easier. Still, he's in jail and will be for the next seven years, pending good behavior.

Which left the problem of me.

Sue stayed in the house with me until this morning, Wednesday, but once it was clear Nigel wouldn't be around for a long time, she pretty much vanished. Hours later, I had a knock at the door. The lady in the flowered pants. Child Services.

Right away I was put into foster care. Where they've sent me is almost too ironic to be real (though I did spend a good half hour begging): 8407 Highcliffe Court.

So here I am. Standing in the foyer like one of my now thirty-eight foster siblings.

Mom takes me by the elbow and guides me toward the living room. "Come on in, Joules. I want you to know you are very welcome here. Whatever issues we had in the past are just that—in the past. We're going to have a fresh start, and everyone's waiting to meet you."

Sure enough, there's Dad with Michaela on his lap, showing her how his watch works, Brayden unraveling the fringe on the sofa cushion, Joules sitting beside him, not swatting the pillow out of his hands when she totally should. Cici and Sam are on the floor, leaning against the sofa, arms hugging their knees. And the Ks—the glorious, chubby, drooling Ks—standing all by themselves in their playpen, holding onto the rail and bopping up and down with delight as they see me.

"Up," Kaia says to me, clearly hoping the new person will be naive enough to free her from her nylon enclosure and let her roam around in search of Play-Doh.

From the rocking chair by the fireplace, Gran winks at me.

Seeing the people in this room, in this house, it's the greatest sight on earth.

"You can call me Lise, and my husband's Gary. Andrea—"

Joules clears her throat loudly and makes a pretend-angry face, and Mom smiles.

"*Andie,* as she likes to be called now, has generously offered to move you into her room, Joules," says Mom, shooting the real Joules an approving look. "You'll be with us a long time, so we've purchased another twin bed, which Gary and Brayden will assemble later tonight. You know Brayden from school, don't you?"

I nod. "Hi, Bray."

"And you're okay sharing a room?"

My room. I'll be back in my room. "Yes. It's perfect. I mean, that'll be fine. Lise." I look around the living room and smile.

I'm back. Not the way I expected, but wishers can't be choosers. I'm not going to be Mom's Number One: I'm not going to be allowed, aside from the odd slip-up, to call her Mom, but still. Here I am, just where I want to be.

Mom instructs Bray to carry my bags into the bedroom and sits me down on the sofa, where I right away try to re-ravel the pillow fringe Bray undid. She explains the deal—Andie is her natural-born daughter. How many fosters they've had over the years. How Bray's been there longer than anyone else. Her belief that this is only the beginning for Joules Adams. I've heard this speech before, but still. It sounds different being directed at me.

To my surprise, Joules leans over and gives me a

hug, and right away I regret not having thought to hug her first. After all, this is easy for me. I'm coming home. Joules is the one who is leaving her life for a while. We hold onto each other as everyone starts to disperse, and Joules whispers to me, "I get it now."

"You get what?" I say.

"Your mom. The kids she brings in. All of it. It's incredible, what she sacrifices. She made a big pot of chili last night and there wasn't enough to go around, so she went without. Made herself a bowl of cereal so none of the fosters had to eat less than a full serving. I could never do what she does."

All these years, I've missed who my parents really are. I've been too focused on what I haven't gotten from them to truly see all they've given up for these kids. And none of it is for *Vanity Fair* magazine or to bolster a failing reputation or to sell more records. It's 100 percent genuine, 100 percent for the kids.

"I know. I knew it before but now I actually see it," I whisper. "She's pretty cool." I watch my dad reach down to wipe drool from Kaia's face and give her nose a little kiss. "They both are."

"Hey, Birch Tree?"

"Yeah?"

"We're friends now, right?"

I nod. "We're friends now."

I can see Mom twisting a Kleenex in her hands. She wants to hug me, Joules, but isn't sure if I'll get all prickly about it. It's tough welcoming the older kids—I know that. Mom wants to be all maternal but holds back at first to assess their needs. But I need nothing if I don't need a hug so I make it easier for her. I stand up and hug her first. With the happiest sad smile you've ever seen, she wraps her arms around me and rocks me back and forth.

I finally understand what it's like to be the foster child. To have Mom fawn all over me and want so badly to erase my ugly past. If this is what every foster kid feels upon coming into this house, they are the lucky ones. Truly.

As for me, I'm lucky to have my mother back.

Like Nigel says, for every itch there's a scratch. And this hug is a scratch I've been wanting for a good long time.

I spend the day hanging with Joules and Bray, who has admitted that ever since Tomas and the others were implicated in the break-and-enter, he doesn't see them any more. Then I hang with Cici and Sam and the Ks. We have Mom's spaghetti for supper. As she's serving, I notice that the tan line where her engagement ring used to be has vanished. As if the ring never existed.

After dinner, as Joules and I are washing the dishes with the yellow Playtex gloves Mom bought to replace Gran's, the doorbell rings. There's a great fuss in the hall—Mom and Gran chatter excitedly to someone we cannot hear. I slip a dry plate into the cupboard and go out into the foyer to find a couple standing with the flowered pants lady.

The man has a bandage wrapped around his head and the woman is in a wheelchair. Adrenaline surges through me as I realize I recognize these two. Here, in my house, are Michaela's parents.

Mom is beaming. She turns to me and says quietly, "Run and get Michaela, Joules, will you? Tell her her parents have come to take her home."

Bray walks past with a textbook in his hand and gives the couple no more than a fleeting glance. He has no idea they're the Disneyland couple. To him, they're just another set of broken parents coming to pick up their child. He's seen it before.

"Joules?" Mom says.

The image of Nigel's SUV, the shattered windshield, won't allow my feet to move just yet. I glance back toward the kitchen, where Joules is still busy at the sink. She has no idea she's fifteen feet away from the family her father nearly destroyed.

I don't have the heart to tell her. Mom's been keeping it hush-hush from all the kids. She's been cryptic with Joules about it. There's a good chance it will never be discussed. There's also a good chance it will. But Joules has been through enough, and it's been a nice evening. She can find out the truth another time.

"Go on, Joules," Mom says with a smile. "Mr. and Mrs. Vikolos are waiting."

I head into the room I now share with Joules and find Michaela sitting like a frog on the floor, humming as she plays with my old stuffed animals. She's wearing the same yellow dress she arrived in. As I squat down beside her I realize she's humming "Rock-a-bye, Baby." The lullaby.

"Michaela, guess who's here?"

She looks up but says nothing.

"Your mom and dad. Want me to take you to see them?"

She nods.

I pick her up—she's light as a piece of paper, for all her dangling limbs. Holding her close, I reach for the stuffed dog she slept with that first night. "You keep him, okay?"

Once again, she nods. But now she has the beginnings of a smile on her lips.

As I head out of the room, I realize I will likely never see her again. I stop, look at her. "I want you to remember something, Michaela. What happened that night happened. It was terrible but it's over. You are not your past. That accident is gone now, okay?"

She stares at me and cocks her head. I wonder if she's detected that I sound like Lise. It's at this moment that I make a decision about my life. I never want to live too far away from this family. I never want to go to Stanford, not when Cal State Fullerton is just down the road.

"You have a great life ahead of you now with your parents," I say to Michaela. "It's all good now. You will never be that alone again."

She studies me a moment and her little chest fills with breath. She reaches up to play with my hair as I take her to where her parents wait.

•

I stand on the darkened front porch for a long time after the Vikoloses' taillights vanish, thinking I'll tell Nigel during visiting hours tomorrow that they're okay now. This couple. He'll be glad of it. Joules is going to come with me. It's the only way she can stay close to him now, through me.

Joules steps out of the house's glow and stands beside me. I notice she's wearing my black sneakers. She pokes me in the side. "Do you want to go back to the bridge again tonight? I'm feeling lucky."

We've been back to look for the gloves half a dozen times. There's never been any sign of them. There will never be any sign of them. The last thing on earth I want to do is go poke around there with flashlights right now.

Gran steps out from behind Joules. "I think it's a good idea. To go to the bridge."

"It's useless," I say. "We've scoured the area. The gloves are gone."

"Maybe you don't need them," says Gran. "Maybe you can make your wish without any gloves at all."

I look at her as if she's insane. Which she clearly is. "We've tried it that way. And under the train. And in a rainstorm. It doesn't work."

Gran steps closer, slightly unsteady from the glass

of wine she had at dinner. There's a mischievous little twinkle in her eye as she pulls something out of her pocket and hands it to Joules. A cloudy hunk of filthy crystal with divots and cracks and not a bit of shine to it. "That same day, I bought the fortune teller's crystal ball."

"Ball?" Joules squints down at it. "More of a crystal rock, isn't it?"

"Looks like you dug it up in the garden," I say as Joules turns it over in her hands. She passes it to me and I hold it up to the light to try and peer into the center, which looks all murky and full of sand.

"What can I say?" Gran shrugs. "I needed a paperweight for my study. But who knows? It might do the trick"

"So do we make the wish here?" asks Joules. "Or go back to the bridge and wait for a train?"

"If you do it here," says Gran, suppressing a smile, "one of you is liable to trade places with Brayden."

Joules grimaces. "We'll go to the bridge."

I wrap my arms around Gran's neck and plant a kiss on her powdered cheek. "You're the best."

She shoves me away, feigning annoyance. "Off with the two of you." She sets her hand over the crystal. "And be careful. That's your last chance you're juggling like that!"

chapter 28

We wrap the crystal rock in one of Sam's leg warmers before climbing out the window. Gran is right; we can't afford to smash this thing. It's not like a roadside fortune teller in Africa would be so easy to find.

It isn't raining tonight, but it's good and dark, and we didn't hear a train as we approached so chances are there'll be one coming along fairly soon. We plop ourselves down in the gravel beneath the bridge, unwrap the crusty little boulder and make a groove for it in the dirt so it doesn't roll away.

"This might not work," says Joules. "We should be prepared for that."

"I know. But whatever happens, it won't be like before. We're too . . . I don't know, interconnected now."

She tucks her hair behind her ears. Then picks at

the stones. "I want you to have him. Whichever way this goes."

"Will?"

"Will."

"You're sure?"

She nods.

I think about this for a moment, hardly daring to breathe. "I kissed him the other day. At school."

"I didn't need to know it, but thanks for sharing."

"Sorry."

"Whatever. It's fine."

"Do you mind if I tell him we're about to switch back?"

She looks at me, incredulous. "He knows about all this? He believed you?"

"Sort of. As much as anyone else can."

"Wow." She throws a pebble toward the street. "You better tell him now, then. Before the train comes."

I pull her phone from my pocket and text Will: About to wish ourselves back again. How would you like to date a girl with 38 siblings?

Just as I slide the phone back into my pocket, the ground begins to rumble.

"Should we hold hands?" Joules asks, scooting closer to the crystal. "Make sure we're touching?"

switch

The original wish was made while I was here and
she was at Will's—a good two miles away—but I
don't point that out. I take hold of her hands and
wait. We stare at each other and blink as the train
gets closer and flecks of debris start to rain down
on us. Joules gets grit on her lip and laughs, spits it
away. We squeeze each other's hands tighter and pull
each other close as the train bursts onto the bridge
and thunders overhead. Then we both say it.

"I wish I was myself again."

chapter 29

I lift my face off the pillow. The sun is out but it's missing the window entirely. Which means I'm facing west. Which means I'm in my old room. But I'm not in the twin bed where Michaela's cot used to be. I'm in my own bed. Which means . . .

I sit up and pull off the covers.

Yes!

Yes!

I am me again! Andrea Birch, for real!

I leap out of bed and look in the mirror, laughing like a crazy person when I see my actual self looking back. And there, in the other bed, is Joules. Sound asleep. I go to wake her but stop when I see the letter from Stanford on my bulletin board. My interview with Mortimer Wolf is today—my last-ditch, if-you-cancel-you-get-no-second-chance interview. If I don't show, I can never apply to Stanford again.

It's okay. Like I said, Cal State Fullerton is just down the street.

A few seconds later, there's a tap at the window.

Will.

I open it up and kneel on the floor so we can be face to face. Our forearms touch, both resting on the sill. Grinning, I say, "It worked, Will! I'm me again."

"I can see that."

"It feels so good. My arms, my legs." *My less cumbersome chest,* I don't say.

"I'm sure."

I tap my pinkie against his. "But weird for you, right? As in, who were you with all this time?"

Will smiles, shakes his head and presses his forehead against mine. "Nope. I know exactly who I was with all this time. I was with Andie Birch."

Andie Birch. The Lucky One.

acknowledgments

Thanks go out . . .

To the two best agents a writer could ask for: the elegant Kassie Evashevski at United Talent Agency and the brilliant Daniel Lazar at Writers House. Kassie, I'm sorry I spilled on your chair. Dan, apologies for all the whining. And fretting. And way-too-long e-mails in the middle of the night, mostly full of whining and fretting.

To my agents' assistants, Dana Borowitz (United Talent Agency) and Stephen Barr (Writers House)—both of whom can answer a question before you ask it. To Maja Nikolic at Writers House for introducing *Switch* to other parts of the globe. To my sensational editors: Lynne Missen at HarperCollins Canada and Greg Ferguson at Egmont USA. To managing editor

Noelle Zitzer and copy editor Catherine Marjoribanks—you made *Switch* a better book. To Regina Griffin and Elizabeth Law at Egmont USA, for being on my side.

To Melissa Zilberberg at HarperCollins Canada for publicity efforts that never stop. To Charidy Johnston and Cory Beatty at HarperCollins Canada for being smart and funny and not losing me in that dark field in Calgary. To Leo MacDonald for supporting my career 1,000 percent.

To Steve for early comments and support. Most of all to Max and Lucas for giving me life.